I0666489

A LITTLE REBELLION...

VAL DUMOND
©2012

MUDDY PUDDLE PRESS

A Little Rebellion…

Published by
Muddy Puddle Press
P O Box 97124
Lakewood WA 98497
www.valdumond.com

ISBN 978-0-9887506-3-0
First Edition
Printed in the United States

Library of Congress Cataloging-in-Publication Data:
Available from publisher
Dumond, Val
A LITTLE REBELLION…
An original novel by Val Dumond
English/Val Dumond
Alphabetic order by last name
ISBN 978-0-9887506-3-0
1. Fiction. 2. Equal rights for women. 3. Women's history.
4. Women's movement. 5. Women in business. 6. Women's rights.

Table of Contents

DEDICATED TO

The Willmar Eight

The brave Minnesota women
who saw the injustice
of gender inequality
in the workplace in 1977
and did something about it

THE STAGE IS SET

A theater is a place where fantasy occurs — in the dark. With the houselights out. The darkness allows spotlights to focus in glittering detail on whatever a playwright chooses. Fact or fiction, real or make-believe — anything is possible in the glaring spotlight in a darkened room.

The performer leads the audience — in laughs, in song, in tears, on trips into worlds of emotions, conflict, and make-believe. The performer leads, has the power, as long as the performer respects the audience and recognizes its power.

The audience, on the other hand, sits in the dark, following the performance, laughing or crying in appropriate places, joining in song, moving along through worlds of fantasy as directed. All continues well, unless the audience is led too far and becomes uncomfortable. Then they rebel.

Sometimes the audience realizes its power and reacts in an unexpected way.

Com'on Bert. Let's pretend you're the kid and I'm...

Aw, Jessica, do I have to?

Yes, Bert. Now I'll be the daddy and I'll come home and...

Hey, you can't. I'll be the dad. I'm the boy...

No, I'll be the daddy; I'm older.

Jess-i-ca! You can't be the dad.

And just why not?

Because... you're a girrll!

That doesn't matter when you're play acting. I can play act at being the daddy. Mommy says so. That's why she named me Jessica — after Jessica Tandy, who can be anything she wants on the stage.

Life Is a TV Commercial

Jessica felt like the actress in the coffee commercial as she padded into the kitchen. She felt the cold floor through her slippers and shivered as she drew water for the coffee maker.

Life is one long commercial, she thought. There's no beginning and no ending. It just goes on and on. See the mother prepare breakfast, a tasty nutritious breakfast for her family. See her prepare aromatic delicious coffee.

As the water started to gurgle, Jessica reached into the refrigerator for a grapefruit and started cutting. "Amy," she called. "Do you want grapefruit or orange? Let's go, Richard, get a move on. The school bus may be early today. The world looks icy."

By talking the day into movement, Jessica began to feel more in control, as if she could push a button and stop the action or push another button and fast forward.

The phone rang. A call before seven has to be *him*. "Hello." She held the phone on her shoulder as she continued sectioning the grapefruit.

"It's me," said the voice. "I'm concerned about the seating arrangement for the big meeting this afternoon. I want you to go down to the theater this morning and check it out yourself."

"Okay." Jessica put down the knife and held the phone with her freed hand. "Before or after the officers' meeting?" she asked trying to sound casual. Damn him! Damn him for interrupting her morning. Damn him for invading her home, her time. Damn him for issuing orders like a commanding general, and for telling her to be in two places at once.

"Come on, Helen. The officers meet at nine; you can be at the theater by ten. You'll have plenty of time."

She hated to be called Helen. He used nicknames because he couldn't remember people's real names. The old coot knew she played in an amateur theater group once, and decided to call her *Helen Hayes*. "It's just that..." Jessica began.

The voice interrupted, "And be sure the scripts are in place. The directors forget them if they aren't on the table."

"Yes, chief." She used her crisp, efficient, I've-got-it-covered office voice. "Everything will go smoothly. Has an annual meeting ever gone anything but smoothly?"

"Let's keep it that way," he said tersely, and hung up.

"Damn!" Jessica blew the word into the kitchen air. "Damn, damn, damn."

"The boss?" Amy asked as she entered the kitchen, grabbed an orange, and began to peel it. "Mom, today I'm going to..."

"Yes, the boss," Jessica spit out the words. "You'd think the annual meeting was an international conference."

"Can't he wait till you get to the office?"

"You know how he likes to throw his weight around. He enjoys watching us jump at his orders." Jessica sighed and sat down at the table with her grapefruit and a bowl of cereal. "Anyway, it's not your worry. Is that all you're eating for breakfast? Where's Rich? Is he coming?"

"He left early for basketball practice or something."

"Do you think you could find time today to dismantle the Christmas garden? It's the middle of January. Time to put it away."

"Yeah, I guess."

"Have Richard help you. He can take down the tree. And make sure he packs the bulbs so they don't break, and wind the tinsel ropes, and..."

"Okay, Mom. We'll do it. Gotta go. See you tonight," called the girl as she pulled her coat from the closet and dashed for the door, waving her coat and clutching her books to her chest.

"Don't forget your scarf. It's cold today."

Jessica poured another cup of coffee for her commercial and shuffled over to the kitchen window, enjoying the warm mug between her hands.

I wonder if Dan's thinking of me over his morning coffee. No, I guess Chicago's business day is already in high gear. Was he really upset last night, or did I imagine the anger? I'd sure love to have him move back out here, but then he'd expect a commitment. I'm just not ready for that.

Ought to finish getting dressed. Wonder if Dan's beginning to sense my situation with Will? He did ask if there was anyone else. I can't tell him about Will... not just yet.

Try to remember, Jess, what did you and Will talk about the last time he was here? Did he say he'd be back in the spring? Or was that wishful thinking? Isn't your life convenient, Jessica Wilson Nadeau? The career woman. Forty-something. Having affairs with two men, both out of town, neither knowing about the other.

She watched the winter robins pecking at the red berries on the sumac tree in the soft morning haze that wasn't quite daylight. Will. Is it Will I love or the idea of loving Will? After all these years. And Dan... sweet sweet Dan. So gentle, so patient, so... where does that leave you, dear Jessica?

Jessica poured another half cup of coffee, turned off the coffee maker, and walked into the living room. The brittle Christmas tree stood in the corner. She could hear the needles dropping on top of the figures in the Christmas garden. She turned on the tree and listened to the electric train hum to life.

"Life used to be so simple, Phil, when you were alive. When it was just you and me and the children," she said aloud. "I'm so glad you told me about the Christmas gardens of Baltimore. Amy makes sure we have one every year. She loves the trains. I do too. I never told you this, but I used to yearn for an electric train of my own. My cousins had them — boy cousins — but I never did. Dad said trains were for boys."

Still talking to her dead husband, Jessica pushed the lever to start the train. "Oh how I loved to handle the controls, those few times they let me. I made sure that Amy got the electric train. It's hers, and she decides who plays with it." She sounded the whistle and watched it move around the track, past the station, through the town. Lights blinked at the crossings; lights shone in the church window; lights flickered on the tree above. She felt like that little girl again.

When the cup in her hand no longer felt warm, she glanced at the clock. The coffee was gone; so was the time.

She turned off the Christmas lights, darted to her bedroom, buttoned herself into a tailored white blouse, wiggled into her navy blue work skirt and blazer, slipped into her navy heels, and raced out the door.

CURTAIN GOING UP

The large blue-black highly-polished sedan pulled into the restricted parking space in front of the dingy theater in downtown Capital City. After a moment, an impressive-looking man in a black business suit stepped into the weak winter sunlight.

Carrying a large black briefcase, Thomas J. Talcott strode through the front door, nodded at the few employees in the lobby and confirmed, "Everybody in place?" Without waiting for a reply, he entered the auditorium and, bald head held high, marched toward the stage, a smile pasted on his face, his hands waving genially at the six shareholders seated to the left of his vice presidents. Nodding to his staff, he shook hands with two of his vice presidents before attempting to hop onto the stage. The portly man in his sixties decided to take the stairs. As he mounted the steps, the last of his employees scurried to their seats.

Seated around the table on stage were the old men who made up the Board, ranging in age from the old-timers at eighty-five to a young newcomer of fifty-nine.

Below, in the front row of the audience, sat the CFO, three senior vice presidents, and six plain VPs, only one of them a woman. Behind them sat the assistant vice presidents and five office managers. Branch managers and heads of various departments were seated in the third row. Moving back were other supervisors and mid-management department sub-heads. And bringing up the rear were the 150 tellers, wearing their light powder blue uniforms. Attendance was mandatory. This was one of very few days in the year that all twenty-nine branches of Stateside Savings Bank were closed. Anyone who noticed that the blue clothes were shaded from light in the back rows to near-black navy in the front row also noticed that the women made up the ranks in the back, while mostly men filled the first few rows.

To the right of the stage, as Corporate Secretary, sat Donna Westerhoff surrounded by piles of folders and holding the agenda on top of a stack of papers that filled her lap.

Jessica was one of the last to scurry into place, choosing a seat on the left aisle, several rows behind the shareholders. She joined Ann Emerson, the boss's private secretary.

"I like to sit back here so I can tell how things are going," Ann whispered to Jessica.

"Sure. I understand. I don't like to get too close to all that hot air either."

"Meeting come to order," Talcott intoned as he rapped his gavel on the bare portable table. "This is the annual shareholders meeting of Stateside Savings Bank, held today, January 17, 1989, called to order at two-oh-three p.m. We'll dispense with the reading of the minutes of the previous meeting... quorum present... initial order of business..."

"How's life in the nether regions?" Jessica asked Ann.

"Not so bad. How's your life going? Have you heard from Dan lately?"

"He was here for Christmas... and we talk on the phone."

"Still haven't made up your mind about him yet, have you?" Ann smiled and scrunched down in the seat.

In voices just above a whisper, the two continued chatting as the bank president conducted his annual shareholders' meeting.

After several minutes of routine business, Jessica leaned back, closed her eyes and muttered to Ann, "Wonder why he bothers with this pomp and circumstance. He sounds like he's conducting a Fortune 500 bank instead of a little twenty-nine-branch outfit. And in this theater! This moldy, colorless, drab place. There sure must be a showman under that bald head, a magician who enjoys performing. But this is ridiculous! Six shareholders and all those cookies out there."

"...my annual address to the shareholders," Talcott's voice boomed out over the speakers.

"His annual address. *His* annual address. I wrote that thing. I write all his speeches, but do I get credit?"

"Careful, Jessica. Someone might hear."

Jessica listened for a moment as the president expounded, "The prospects for the future appear bright. Stateside officers work diligently day and night to assure our shareholders…"

"Diligently? Doesn't he mean desperately? dejectedly? defiantly? depressed? dissatisfied?"

"Are you? Dissatisfied?"

"Well, no, not exactly. I like what I'm doing, my work. I just don't like working for him. How do you stand it… so close to him?"

"I decided early on, that if I was to work for Mr. Talcott, I'd have to develop a skin thicker than his and a sense of who is cowering under that toughness. I've done both."

"You mean, you think he isn't tough?"

"I know. But, shhh. Listen to what he's saying."

"I don't have to. I wrote the words that he's butchering." In unison with the president on the stage, she whispered, "And onward and upward will sail the good ship Stateside Savings."

The president paused for an applause that started small and grew as staffers woke up to the fact he was waiting for it.

"You wrote that?" Ann's eyebrows went up with her voice.

"Yes… and no. You see, I realized that if I were to work with him I'd have to use his words. I just connect them with mine. Look at those old geezers up there. The Bleeper gavels them to order, they read their scripts, then take their little naps."

"I wish you wouldn't call him that. I'm afraid I'm going to blurt it out one day in front of him."

"Sorry." Jessica removed her glasses and closed her eyes to listen.

"…but I can't take the credit for the good news this year. I have to give much of the credit to our loyal employees." He waved his hand across the darkness in front of him.

"Loyal. Sure, loyal peons, flunkies, us little people sitting out here in our blue heaven and smiling adoration on our leader."

"Watch it, my friend. You're talking to one of those loyal flunkies."

"I don't care much anymore. I'm getting sick and tired of being at his call twenty-four hours a day. Do you know he called me at home again this morning? Just to be sure we had all the proxy cards ready."

"I get calls at home too. That's just his way."

"Ann, look up front, on the stage, in the front rows. What do you see?"

"I don't know what you mean."

"Maybe I should ask what don't you see." Jessica waited a moment for Ann to catch on.

"I'm not sure…"

"Sex. Or rather, gender. Look up there. All men."

"Yes? So?" Ann studied Jessica's face.

"How come we don't have women on our Board of Directors? How come there's only one woman among the vice presidents?"

"The question of women on the Board has come up a couple times."

"I remember, about three years ago. A shareholder asked about electing women to the Board. Whatever happened to that idea?"

"The usual, Jessica. You know how he answers questions like that. 'That's a good suggestion. We'll take it under consideration'."

"We know where considerations end up, don't we. Do you think there ever will be women up there?"

"Not while Mr. Talcott's alive," Ann smiled. "You know his three big hang-ups…"

The two chanted in whispers, "Coffee, cigarets, and chicks in the business office."

"Still, we do have coffee in the cafeteria, and smoking in the lounge," Ann offered.

"And 'chicks' in business. But look at *them*. Look where they sit. They're mostly tellers. A few branch managers and a couple assistant vice presidents — in name — like me. Only Sheila is up there with the VPs. And we know she got the title because she's a friend of the family."

"And Donna. She's the corporate secretary."

"With the accent on *secretary*. She's supposed to be a Board officer, but he won't let her sit on the stage or vote as a member of the Board."

"Technically she's not a member. She's a bank officer."

"God you're picky, Ann. No wonder you make a good secretary to him."

"Call for the Proxy Committee Report," the president read from his agenda. When he received no response, he repeated, louder, "Call for the Proxy Committee Report. The Proxy Committee."

Board member Anderson prodded Mr. Owens with his elbow. "Oh, oh, all right," Owens mumbled as he shuffled the papers in front of him. "Report of the Proxy Committee shows, uh, er…" He finally pulled out a page and read, "77,256 eligible member votes, proxies of 69,815 on file, counted through proper audit."

"And every single one collected and verified by me," whispered Jessica. "I collected every one of those little permission slips that decide how the votes are cast. Just look: only six real live voters here. That leaves 77,250 votes for the committee to control. It's so simple. Get your name on the Proxy Committee and you can cast those votes too."

Ann patted Jessica's arm and kept her eyes on the stage.

"Did you hear what I just said, Ann?" Jessica who had been lounging in her seat sat up straight. "Get your name on the Proxy Committee and…" She shuddered and looked around in the half-light at the audience.

"Whoa!" said Ann as she caught Jessica's implication. "You're reaching into fantasyland now." But Jessica's head reeled with what began to dance inside. "What if…" she dared, "What if a woman's name were on those proxies? What if you and I were on that Proxy Committee?"

"No way," Ann answered. "Remember, the Board chooses the committee, and there aren't women on the Board. Sorry, Jess, you'll have to come up with something better to do with *your* proxy cards." Jessica slumped back into the seat.

Then another thought erupted. "*My* proxy cards. My... proxy... cards. Mine!" Her lips formed the words and she looked around again. Had she spoken too loud? But everyone else's attention was directed at the business onstage.

Her spirits rose as she asked Ann, "What if we made up a whole new Proxy Committee with women on it? What if we brought our own proxy cards to the annual meeting and cast our own votes for a woman to sit on the Board?"

"Where do you get the *we*, Jessica? You couldn't do this alone. You'd have to have help. And who would stick their neck out to get a woman on the Board?"

Jessica replaced her glasses and looked around the group that stared up at the lighted stage. "Sheila McDowell, the aging leading lady?" she asked. "Sheila's smart and experienced. Look at how well she fits in the front row with those top execs. She knows investments like nobody else."

"Sorry, Jess, she's too close to retirement to risk it all. Besides, she's also too close to the Talcotts."

Back on stage, Talcott asked, "Corporate Secretary, can you verify the proxy count?"

"Verified," repeated Donna.

"How about Donna Westerhoff, the supporting player?" whispered Jessica. "She already knows all there is to know about the Board and how it operates. She could run this bank by herself. Hell, she does it when the Bleeper is out of town... sorry... when Mr. Talcott is out of town."

"No. She keeps telling me, 'I'd rather be near power than have it'. What's more, she seems to shake at the idea of moving any closer than she is."

Jessica continued her search, settling her gaze on Winnie Flemming and Terri Litton-Clark, scrunched down in their seats and giggling behind cupped hands.

"Look there," she mumbled to Ann. "Winnie Flemming, starlet or chorus girl? She manages an entire department, but she doesn't seem the corporate type — swings her hips too much, worries more about her hair than the bank."

"She's not over her divorce. She's still dealing with her husband leaving. No, she's not leadership material yet." Was Ann joining Jessica's fantasy?

Jessica closed her eyes for a moment and saw herself just after Phil died. Too much makeup, garish vests worn over see-through blouses with tight hip-hugger pants. The discos and frantic dancing, always looking for another Phil, a special someone who could make it all better. "Winnie's doing the best she can for now," she told Ann.

"How about Terri Litton-Clark?" suggested Ann. "The ingénue who's a leader. She can wind people around her fingers like so many puppet strings. I've watched her do it with Talcott. MBA. Definitely the career type. Maybe one day… young married…"

"Has she made it legal yet with her live-in friend?" Jessica asked. "I'll bet she and Winnie are talking about a new male stripper or something."

A movement across the aisle caught Jessica's eye. Judy Robertson flipped over the page of her yellow note pad and smiled as she continued her scribbling. "My god, she even works during the annual meeting." Jessica nearly forgot to whisper. "Old nose-to-the-grindstone Judy, like an ambitious understudy. I talked to her once about her busy-ness, and Judy said she didn't realize how much she worked. She said it felt good, and besides, she was worried that if she didn't work hard enough she would be replaced. 'Maybe if I learned a new job, transferred to another department, became indispensable someplace else…' was the way she put it."

"A possibility," agreed Ann. "Judy's good at taking notes, planning projects, making herself indispensable. She knows every section of the bank… calls it job security… but she'd never believe she could become a Board member."

"I think her lack of self confidence comes from that overbearing boorish husband of hers. He doesn't let her move without his approval."

"That completes the re-election of officers," Talcott announced. "And that completes this year's business for the annual meeting. The Board of Directors will hold an organizational meeting tomorrow morning. We wish to greet the shareholders here today. Thank you for coming. There are refreshments in the lobby."

As tersely as he began, Talcott now concluded the meeting by ceremoniously bringing down the gavel on the rickety table and intoning, "Meeting adjourned."

"How about you, Jessica?" Ann whispered to her friend.

Startled, all Jessica could think of was, "No, no, no, no no! Definitely no. I'd love to see it happen, but not me. I'm not in the banking business for life."

As the theater lights came up, Ann could see Jessica more clearly. She was gripping the arms of her seat as she mulled over their ideas. "If everyone worked together... an intriguing idea. What if everyone were to join forces?" Neither of the women moved as the audience stood up. "What if all the women working at the bank were to work as a solid unit... solidarity... the word has the distinct ring of freedom and independence and throwing off shackles." She gripped the arms even tighter to keep from shouting. Ann could feel her excitement.

"You know, Ann, there's a kind of irony about holding this meeting here in this old theater. The lights accent those shabby drapes, the worn seats, the dingy walls. This place looks tattered in the bright light, but remember how luxurious those drapes looked in the dark. The boss does a kind of sleight of hand here, doesn't he? His own kind of flimflam."

"But this is the reality, the light," returned Ann. "Dingy curtains, musty walls, worn seats, and all."

The women joined the blue wave moving up the aisle. Jessica looked down. "Even the carpet is thread-bare."

The meeting adjourned and Jessica's daydream was put on hold.

In the brighter lights of the lobby, the bank employees and the six shareholders milled about, sipping hot coffee and eating cookies. One eager young man in the navy blazer and gray pants uniform approached the president and cooed, "Nice speech, Mr. Talcott."

"Thank you, er…" the president paused in mid-chew of his chocolate cookie to read the young man's name tag, "Adams. How's the family, Adams?"

Ann moved toward her boss to congratulate him.

Jessica nudged Sheila, who stood presiding over the refreshment table. "Something out of whack here," she said. "I wrote that speech, but I don't get the credit. You're a vice president and he has you pushing cookies. Is that because we're women?"

"At least I'm pushing something," Sheila shot back, then coughed. "The mildew and dust are getting to me. I'll be glad to get out of here." She looked up to see Mr. Talcott in front of her and shifted into a smile, "Hi, boss, nice speech."

Jessica glared at Sheila and calmly told her boss, "Good meeting, Mr. Talcott."

"Thanks, girls. Now, how about you…" he took Jessica's arm and steered her toward the door, "…get back to the office and prepare those public relations notices."

"No need, Mr. Talcott," she told him proudly. "The press packages are ready for the media; they're on your desk." What a heady feeling to be one step in front of him for a change.

"Uh, I've thought up another approach. I want those releases to play up the fact that I've been elected president for the eighteenth successive year. You'll have to re-write the leads this afternoon."

"Of course, Mr. Talcott," Jessica began lamely as her boss walked away. "I'll get them out this evening. Good idea." Her smile remained frozen, along with the blood in her body. She turned to Sheila and glared, her insides dry and cold. "If I didn't need this miserable job, I'd quit right this minute. Why couldn't he have told me that yesterday? Wasn't he sure he'd be re-elected? He does this to me all the time, waits until I have a job completed, then tells me he's changed his mind. I shouldn't even be surprised anymore. Damn! Damn! Double damn!"

"Jess. How long have you been marketing director? Four… five years? You should have learned by now that you can't outguess the boss. He carries the ball and tosses it around whenever and wherever he darned pleases."

"It's just that I thought… this time… this time…." Jessica's shoulders dropped. She looked spent. "I swear he gets his kicks watching us squirm." She wanted to stamp her feet, but she fought the urge. "Guess I'd better get back to the office or I'll be working all night."

Back at her desk, she turned on the word processor, pulled the press releases from the packets and began to re-type the lead. She didn't waste much time on it — she'd done this before. As she watched her work shoot out of the copier, she returned to her talk with Ann and the idea they both considered a fantasy.

What would it be like to write a speech for a woman bank president? The only one I know of heads that woman's bank in Seattle. How would it be to work for her? Surely, no woman would conduct business with the paranoia that the Bleeper does. I've never worked for a woman boss.

One day, some day, a woman will stand before that sleepy old Board of Directors. Who? Would she have to be as gutsy, as shrewd, as heartless, as cold and mechanical as the Bleeper? Would she have to put up with those old codgers on the Board? Or could she be a woman who understands and enjoys working with people? Could she be a woman who would lead and instruct and draw good people around her? Could a woman do this and keep the bank profitable? Was there a way to make good leadership equate with balanced ledgers? Was there such a woman in the whole world?

"Who's there?" she called as she heard the elevator door.

"Just me Winnie," returned the answer. "Came to see if you need help." Winnie swung around the corner and took off her coat.

"I'm almost finished," Jessica told her friend.

"Why don't you quit? I see how angry you are. He shouldn't treat you this way. Hell, he shouldn't treat any of us this way."

"Sometimes I wonder too. Why should I just *get through* my days?" Jessica scooped up a set of papers and handed them to Winnie to be stapled.

"But you have so much to offer."

"I'm getting older, nearly forty."

"Couldn't you get back into television?" asked Winnie.

"Maybe, but I'd have to start at the bottom again. If I had stayed at the television station, I know I could have worked up to reporter to… who knows how far I might have soared? And then again, maybe there's a Bleeper at the head of the station. You never know."

"He treats you so… so…"

"Oh, it's not all that bad. As long as the children are young, I need to continue to move toward some kind of career. At this moment, advertising and public relations are my strengths. I also know that as good as I am at this job, I could… he could… well, you know. The truth is I need the job."

The two gathered the papers from the copier and moved back toward Jessica's office.

"The Bleeper knows how badly we all need our jobs," Winnie said. "We're not the only ones." As they walked down the hall, Winnie pointed to the office of one of the vice presidents. "He has a drinking problem." They passed a closed door and she pointed again, "He was merged out of the bank he directed and was grateful for his position here. It's like that with most of us. We owe him."

"You're right," Jessica said. "Most of the women are divorced, widowed, or otherwise dependent upon their jobs for their livelihoods. And those poor tellers, literally poor, living on their minimum wages."

"Talcott has a knack for picking up people when they're down, when they would welcome a job, any kind of a job at any kind of pay. He gives it to them, and in return they gave him a kind of loyalty."

"Don't I know!" Jessica stopped to juggle her press releases. "When I started here, I'd have traded anything for a job." They walked in silence for a moment, then, "It sure would be fun to put one over on him."

"What do you mean?" Winnie slung her coat over her shoulders and followed Jessica around the corner to her office.

"Oh nothing, just something I can have fun thinking about. Someday." She swept her desk clear, replacing books on the shelf and tossing papers in drawers (clear desk tops were a company rule). The pink telephone memo with Dan's name on it caught her eye, and she lifted it carefully out of the stack, read it, and placed it in her purse.

"Gotta get home. Dan's going to call tonight. And thanks for the help, Winnie."

The lights in her office flicked out just past seven thirty.

JESSICA

Jessica backed the car out of the bank parking lot and maneuvered through the dark streets. She rolled down the window and took a deep breath of the crisp winter air. No sign of a January thaw, let alone spring. Easing onto the freeway, she slipped off her shoes and tossed them in the back. Then she rolled up the window and let out an expansive scream, moving on to yells of epithets, cuss words, every nasty phrase she had ever heard, adding a few of her own.

"Simpering, egotistical idiot! Stupid, moronic jerk! Why do I let that overbearing maniac ruin my life! Why do I put up with his degrading, demeaning, denigrating, patronizing…" She continued screaming for nearly eight minutes, until she ran out of words… and steam.

"Wow, bad day. Screamed past four exits. This month's record. Nearly home now."

Home. After each workday, Jessica tried to switch off her work brain and kick in her home brain during the twenty-minute drive. Now, leaving the furies of the day behind her, she turned onto the exit ramp and into the quiet streets. Again she rolled down the window and breathed deeply, noticing a distinct clearing of her head.

Now she could begin thinking about home and what waited for her. Her son Richard should be home from basketball practice by now; it's nearly eight. And Amy would be there, keeping her supper warm, ready with a neck massage. My dear Amy, how unlike herself as a ten-year-old.

As a girl, Jessica used to play with the boys, or tried to. They didn't let her in much of the time. Jess could never understand why little girls didn't play with the fun things that boys did — tree houses, train sets, bicycles, baseball. If only she had been born a boy. She might be president of the damn bank by now instead of….

She swung the car around a corner and talked to herself as she waited to make a left turn. "Face it, Jess. To have any power you have to be a man. You've heard it for thirty-hmm years. Why won't you believe it, accept it, move on? I won't, I won't, I won't," she answered herself. "I can't accept that. I won't." She was talking to no one, everyone.

"You'd be doing something useful now, something important if you'd been born male — like your parents wanted. Like everybody wanted. Wouldn't that be a gas? All male babies. The perfect world! You're thinking crazy. You're very tired. That old poop really did a number on you today, just when you thought you had it all locked up."

Still there was the evening to face — and Dan. He's going to call tonight and I don't feel like being nice. Maybe he'll do the talking and won't notice my mood. I don't want to argue togetherness tonight. Not yet. I like my life the way it is.

Jessica steered the car down the cul-de-sac that led to her house. Every time she thought of the options, she settled on the good feeling she had with her life now — head of the house, a mother with a good job, in charge of her life, at least at home.

Her two-part conversation with herself continued as she glided into the driveway.

"Isn't that strange, Jess, how you just listed *head of the house* as the best part of your life? Head of the house, that's a man's job. But then, what isn't? A man can have any job he wants...."

"...except that of mother," she interrupted herself with the joke that brought a smile to her face at last. "That's a woman's only real power, being a mother, or just knowing she can be a mother."

The lights were on all over her house as she maneuvered into the garage, turned off the motor, and waited for the automatic door to close. She liked this part best, the aroma of Amy's supper preparations meeting her in the garage. She poked around the backseat until she found her shoes, then put them on, picked up her briefcase, and walked slowly into the kitchen.

"You look ragged, Mom," Richard noticed.

"Thanks, son, are you trying to get on my better side to borrow the car or do you have a report card for me to sign?" Richard, almost fourteen, was tall and gangly, and looked very much like a basketball player.

"Naw, you just look zonked." Then, "Can I? Borrow the car?"

"Sure, in two years. But thanks for noticing." She always felt lucky to have a son who was sensitive to her moods. Most of the time, anyway. He had his bad moments, and she attributed the temper outbursts to teenage hormones. Periodically, every few months, his anger would well up and overtake his good nature, turning him into this male monster that had to be in control of his space — and hers. She felt his natural urge to become the man of the house, to assert his control over her, and run things his way. She had found that the only way to deal with him at those times was to physically overtake him, show him her strength by refusing to be pushed around, and return his hurtful words with understanding. He seemed to want this to happen, to be relieved of some burden he had placed on himself.

It worked. But lately, she was finding it more difficult to physically overpower him. He already was taller than she. The last time he blew up at her was just before Christmas. The combination of pre-holiday stress, Dan's visit, and the built-in pressure of a teenager had fused to bring on the explosion. Jessica took his abusive words, his put-downs, slurs and then outright profanity for about three days before he began to cross her line, a more lenient line than most parents would allow. Jessica gave him room to stretch his emotions. The confrontation began when he physically cornered her in the hallway, pushing her against the wall. She elbowed him away and followed him into his room. He glowered at her and lashed out with his hand.

They both recognized the boundary; both knew it had been crossed. "Enough, young man," she yelled. "That's far enough." When he pushed her again, she grabbed his arm, held it tightly, swung him around, and pinned his arm against his back. Squirm as he did, she managed to hold on, using all her strength. She lifted the arm slowly, until his knees buckled with the pressure and he was down.

She felt the release of his antagonism. More important, she felt his relief at knowing Mom was still in charge. But she didn't waste time talking to him then. She made sure he knew who was the head of her house, and then left him alone. She knew he would come to her later and apologize, another crisis met and passed. Still, she dreaded the next time. He was getting so strong.

Tonight he was happy, his old joking self. The kid had a wonderful way of memorizing comedy routines and could mimic Robin Williams better than anyone she knew. She loved his sense of humor, the way he enjoyed making her laugh.

"Well, if I can't have the car, I'll go hit the books," Richard said, tossing a salute as he left the room.

Amy was busy at the stove, pulling something from the oven. "Biscuits, oh you darling," the mother praised her young daughter. "What's my surprise tonight?" The two had discovered the best way to handle evening meals was to stock up on prepared dinners and have Amy plunk them in the microwave when she heard the car drive up. That way, nobody suffered through meals gone cold or spoiled preparations. Jessica always pretended not to recognize the meal she had collected at the grocery. And since Amy made the evening selection, there was a kind of surprise element to Jessica's meals.

"Chicken Kiev!" Amy proudly set the warm plate in front of her mother. She had transferred the dinner from the carton to the dinner plate to make room for the biscuits.

"Oh, I need something special tonight." She hugged her daughter and kicked off her shoes at the same time. "Thanks, darling. How'd your day go? Did you get the Christmas garden packed up?"

"Not quite. I'll finish this evening."

Amy began to recount her day at school. Jessica stood up and removed her glasses as she unbuttoned her blouse and skirt. She asked Amy to hold her thought while she disappeared into the bedroom and slipped out of her clothes. In almost a single movement, she slid into a sweatsuit and removed the pins from her hair. She shook her head as she re-entered the kitchen.

Amy continued relating her adventures of the day while Jessica ate her chicken dinner, along with three biscuits. Amy distractedly spread jam on a biscuit and munched on it while she explained about the new project her class was starting. Jessica followed as long as she could, then her attention roamed to Dan and his expected call.

"Will you come?" she heard Amy ask a few moments later. "Will you, Mom?"

"Huh, oh yes, of course I will, sweetheart," she responded, not sure what she had committed to. "Just remind me."

The two cleared the dishes and filled the dishwasher. Jessica usually enjoyed this time with her daughter, but tonight she felt slightly distracted.

"Mom, how come we don't sing together anymore?"

"Huh? What do you mean?"

"You know. Sing, like 'Let The Sunshine In', like we used to."

"I don't know," Jessica answered. "It *has* been awhile since I've sung with you."

"You have such a good voice. Rich says you used to sing a lot when he was little."

"Things were different then, pumpkin. Things were very different when your father was alive. I guess I kind of lost my voice after he died."

"Oh." Amy poured out the detergent and emptied it into the dishwasher. As she closed the door, she wrapped her arms around her mother. The two embraced, quietly, feeling their shared loss.

Amy walked off to watch a re-run of "The Cosby Show" and pack up the train set, and Jessica pulled open her briefcase. She took out the first draft of the new ad campaign and tried to work on it, but soon let it fall to her lap as her eyes closed momentarily.

"It *has* been awhile since I've sung. Not even in the shower. Funny Amy would say that tonight. I don't even…"

The ringing phone interrupted. "It's for you, Mom," called Richard from the next room. "It's Dan." Jessica could hear her son talking to her friend as she padded barefoot down the hallway to her bedroom. "I'll take it in here," she called to Richard.

"Hi, you," she spoke softly into the phone. "How are things in Chicago?"

"Oh you sound tired," came the response. "The old man getting to you?"

DAN

Dan's voice always sounded like a soothing ointment to Jessica's bruised heart. He always seemed to know just the right things to say, and always at the right moment. His timing was perfect.

An old friend from college in Milwaukee, Dan Weldon had shown up again in Jessica's life through one of those freak accidents that life tosses in. When they re-met on that plane two years ago, she was dealing with nearing forty and recently widowed, concentrating on her career, not on her love life.

Dan was changing direction back then too. After his divorce, he was taking a look at career opportunities in other directions. In fact, the plane trip was to interview with a mid-west publisher. Dan and Jessica spotted each other immediately and gasped over the coincidence as the plane headed east across Nebraska. She had talked the boss into letting her attend a marketing convention in Chicago and was anticipating a few days of freedom and fun alone. Dan Weldon climbed aboard her plane in Portland and back into her world. By the time the plane landed in Chicago, they had re-established contact, exchanged addresses and phone numbers, and made plans to meet after their respective Chicago events.

They had spent a wonderful few days together, before returning to their old worlds to contemplate what had happened. Over the next two years, he called her on a somewhat regular basis, and they'd rendezvous as often as they both could get away.

Back in college, Jessica and Dan were only casual acquaintances. Neither remembers if they ever dated. Now the friendship seemed stronger just because they had been apart so long and still once shared that time and place together.

Permanent relationship? Neither was strong enough to make that commitment. Both were still hurting too much from their own ended marriages. Neither was ready for permanent togetherness, and they were smart enough to know it. Jessica felt she'd know what to do if he ever made a move towards marriage, but as yet she hadn't wanted to acknowledge it.

They talked about it briefly when Dan visited last fall and again at Christmastime. But all they managed to do was raise the questions — the problems that needed to be solved if they ever decided to live together.

Where would they live? He had his grand new job in Chicago. She had her career underway in the Northwest; she had invested five years in it and wouldn't give up her comfortable salary without a good reason. If she moved there, it would mean looking for a new job, uprooting the children. Would any of his children live with him… them? He had two daughters, twelve and fourteen, and a sixteen-year-old son. How would they work out with her Richard and Amy?

Now, after two years of talking and laughing and loving, they chatted casually about his work and the weather. Jessica liked talking to this man. She never felt pushed or apprehensive. After several minutes they paused in their conversation and just enjoyed being connected. When such silences occurred, they both listened to the humming space between them and the "just being there".

After a moment, Dan asked, "Jess, have you thought more about joining me here?"

Another pause before, "Dan, I don't know. Yes, I've thought about it. Of course I have, but I can't decide. I have a good job here, a kind of investment in my career. Still, you know I love you and would like to join you there." She drew a deep breath, "Have you thought any more about our kids? Are yours with you yet, or did they go back to their mother?"

"They were here for New Years, and they've gone back. School, you know. But they're asking to come live with me next summer and maybe stay on when school begins in the fall. You see, Jess, we'd be a real family."

Jessica had known too many friends who had pushed their families together, his and her kids. Usually it didn't work; occasionally it worked after a long period of adjustment. But it was never easy.

"I wouldn't want to move my children right now in mid-term either. But maybe next summer… tell you what, Dan. Let's keep things as they are right now, and we can come to a decision over the summer."

Jessica left the subject unanswered; Dan let the subject drop; this was a topic that would come up again and again before it would be decided. Both of them kept hoping some outside element would resolve their dilemma, something neither of them had counted on. Nothing had come along so far, but maybe, just maybe.

Boss Talcott

The drive to work the next day ran the film in reverse of the drive home. She tried to use the time to put her home behind her and plan the workday. "Plan! Ha!" she laughed aloud. "Like you can plan when you work for the Bleeper!" She swung the car around a poky driver and back into her lane.

Jessica had worked for Mr. Talcott long enough to notice some of his impatience rubbing off on her. She hated driving slow and standing in lines; she demanded her space and immediate service. She expected things to happen right away, as soon as she asked. Her children hated it; maybe Talcott's kids did too.

Dan hated it, she knew. Jess hadn't slept much last night reliving the evening just before Christmas when Dan arrived from Chicago. It had started badly when she ordered Dan to pick her up at the office because her car was acting up. Events continued downhill as she insisted on talking incessantly about her work. She didn't even notice the perfectly good dinner Dan had ordered because she was talking about "the office".

"Poor Dan," she murmured. "He's such a good sport and I treat him like a flunky hired to take me out to dinner." Still, she needed him. And now she seemed to be doing everything wrong. She knew she was pushing him away, pretending to put her work first, pretending to get on without him very well. She had survived Phil's death, after all, for many years without a knight on a white horse. Then along came Dan, riding up to rescue her, just like in the movies. Now, to her surprise, she was holding him off, refusing to tie herself to a commitment.

"Why can't I just accept the happily-ever-after ending of the silver screen?" she asked. "What's holding me back? Why can't I make up my mind?"

By the time she arrived at the office, she had switched her thoughts to the day ahead, and began by recalling the annual meeting and her wild ideas. "Why is it that yesterday's dreams seem so futile in daylight?" she asked herself. "Your own proxy committee? Not bloody likely."

The phone rang and she picked it up. "Boss wants to see you, Jessica," she heard Ann's soft voice.

"Be right there," Jessica cooed back. "Wonder what he wants now. He can't re-call the press releases; I've already mailed them."

She gathered up a notepad and pen and headed for the president's suite. Ann greeted her as she rounded the corner.

"He's with somebody now; said to wait."

"Any idea what's up?"

"The usual. Everything and nothing."

"I'd have thought he'd be busy getting ready for the Board. They'll be here in an hour or so, won't they?"

"Is today the day after the annual stage show?"

The buzzer sounded on Ann's desk and she responded. "Okay, I'll send her in." She nodded at Jess.

"Morning, Mr. Talcott," Jessica greeted her boss as she entered the leathery inner office. The corner office on the top floor of the building commanded a wide panorama of Puget Sound. If she wanted to, she could watch the boats gliding in and out of the marina just below, or follow the paths of the seagulls searching for their breakfasts.

Mr. Talcott didn't raise his head as he motioned her to sit. Sitting down was a bad sign he was going to dictate one of his ideas-while-shaving. She walked past the over-stuffed sofa, took her place on the straight chair, clicked her pen to attention and waited as he shuffled through a stack of papers.

"Friday," he called out the open door. "Friday, come get this." When his secretary Ann appeared, he tossed some papers at her with the directions, "Take these over to Personnel. Don't know why this stuff comes to me."

Ann left and Talcott returned to his stack for several more minutes, jotting notes on one page, crumpling another, marking still another with a huge X and shoving it aside. "No, no, no," he muttered. Jessica was beginning to catch his mood — not good at all.

The portrait of the Senior Talcott stared at her from the wall behind her boss's desk. Word was he hung it behind him so he wouldn't have to look at it. The other walls bore elegant paintings of sailing vessels from long ago. The scowling portrait of the Senior Talcott, who had founded the company and set its course, looked just like his son, the current president and chairman of the Board.

The two Talcotts not only looked alike — both were bald, had narrow eyes and grim lips — but they acted alike — loud, dictatorial and squeaky when angry. And they both had a natural flair for predicting the future and guiding the bank around market crashes and through alternating depressions and inflations. Talcott Senior even predicted his own death, naming his son to succeed him as chairman of the Board at the annual meeting just before he died. "Nice timing," thought Jessica when she read about that chain of events in some old Board minutes.

It was twenty years ago that Junior Talcott had taken over the bank, then a savings and loan, from his dad. Those had been the days when a foreclosure was only a threatened disaster, one that rarely happened. Now, with the business leaning more to the investment side, he had to get tough once in a while to keep the books balanced. While the company's management considered him shrewd, some (former) customers — the victims of foreclosed mortgages — thought him heartless. At this moment, Jessica was beginning to sense some of that *heartless*.

Talcott dropped his pencil to the desk and leaned back in his high-backed executive chair. "Mail, mail, mail," he sighed. "Don't know why it all ends up here." Jessica knew. She could have told him that it was because he ordered all mail to be cleared by him.

Instead she said, "This year's meeting went pretty well," and thought, *without a hitch; nobody brought up any new business; no unforeseen occurrences arose; no reporters showed up.*

"Uh, yeah. And the new Board will be meeting in…" he consulted his desk clock…"forty-eight minutes. I need a promotion to knock their sox off. Something to play up the wavering Money Market rates and get minds off the sinking mortgage rates."

Jessica's mouth dropped. Was he asking her to prepare an ad campaign in forty-eight minutes?

"Need some catchy words. You know the kind, 'it's not a tax break, it's an investment'. Or, 'invest your funds in a trustworthy market'. You know the kind of words that get the attention. We'll need a rough draft print ad, sample radio spots, and an idea for television... the usual."

"In forty-eight minutes?" Jessica sputtered.

"Naw, take the morning," he smiled grandly. "I'll put you on the docket right after lunch." He leaned over his desk again and picked up his pencil, preparing to return to work. Jessica sat tight in her chair. He looked up and dismissed her with, "You've got the assignment. See you at one-thirty. No, better come by at noon and help Donna with the lunches."

She was dismissed. Her head pounded as she rose and staggered out of the office. Rough draft of print ads, commercials, and entire promotional campaign before noon!

As if shocked by a bolt of electricity, she flew down the hall to her office, half-closed the door and grabbed the phone. "May-day, May-day," she called into it after a few moments. "Need your help... new campaign... the works... you know the way he does it." A pause, then, "don't laugh — before noon?"

Jessica and the graphic artist were putting their heads together a few minutes later at his shop down the street. They had gone through these assignments before. More than once, at the whim of her boss, they had put together whole packages in a day or two. But this was different. Two hours. At least they'd give it a shot. Maybe something would come out.

They worked quickly, using the suggestions Talcott had made. "Weak premise," Jessica admitted, "but you know how he likes to hear his words tossed back at him." By eleven forty-five they had everything but the television storyboards. "Can you draw them up and send them over before one?" Jessica asked. Then, bowing, she repeated the boss's request for her waitressing services. "Gotta go serve lunch. And thanks — again."

Outside the Board Room, Donna and Ann were separating the various lunches the caterer had delivered. Jessica pitched in and, when the old men opened the hallowed doors to take their lunch break, the women distributed the lunch boxes around the table. The men all headed for the men's room.

"Oh, by the way," Talcott called over his shoulder to Jess. "Won't be needing that campaign. Haven't time today. Save it for next week."

Somehow Jessica kept her cool. This had happened so often before, she wasn't surprised, just exasperated.

"What was that all about?" Donna asked.

"Don't ask," Jessica responded. "Tell you about it later."

Jessica greeted the artist at the elevator at one o'clock and accepted his storyboards. She hadn't the heart to tell him of Talcott's postponement. She filed the campaign to await Mr. Talcott's next whim. Three months later, he still hadn't asked for the work.

Secretaries' Day

Secretaries' Day is celebrated in April in the business world with the same enthusiasm as President's Day. It takes on a kind of forced warmth reminiscent of smiling while you eat liver at the home of a dear friend.

Talcott's secretary, Ann Emerson, was a stereotypical picture of office efficiency. She wore her wavy hair short, Peter Pan collars, very modest makeup, and a perpetual smile. That April morning she placed a discreet reminder in the stack of her boss's mail — a flier printed by the local Professional Secretaries Association declaring, "Take Your Secretary To Lunch Day".

Ann didn't expect lunch; she just wanted to see The Bleeper's reaction. She took a secret delight at watching him squirm on occasions like this. Curiosity about what made her boss tick was probably what kept her in the job that so many had held for brief periods before her. Working with him was an experience in patience, supplication, stone-skinned-ness and… yes, curiosity. Ann used her avid interest in pop psychology to provide a way to make this a *study* situation and cope with the day-to-day ups and downs of her position.

She delivered his mail and sat down with her steno pad to await his replies. He held up the flier, smiled, and said, "Ha! Great idea. Okay, Friday, why don't you make reservations at the Pacific Lounge for noon today. I'd be delighted to take a pretty girl to lunch. In fact, why not bring along Sheila… and, er, Jessica, Donna, and Winnie and uh, what's her name, Julie…"

"Do you mean Judy?" Ann asked, innocently. He never would remember her name. He was terrible with everyone's name and usually covered it up by using nicknames or none at all. Even Ann's simple name was not in his memory. If he called her anything, it was *Friday,* as in *his girl Friday.*

"Yes, Judy. She ought to be good for some laughs."

Before the morning mail was finished, Terri stuck her head in the door and asked about the day's investment interest rates. "Hey, Blue Eyes," he called to her after Ann had provided the numbers, "how about celebrating Secretaries' Day with lunch today — the Pacific, at noon." He certainly was in a good mood.

Ann added Terri's name to her list, and mentally noted that while he included women with administrative jobs, two bona fide administrative secretaries were not included. She wondered why not, but didn't ask. She had learned not to question his choices. These plunges into civility, like taking a secretary to lunch, so baffled Talcott that he either ignored them or, like today, made an irrational display. No need to question why he had included in his invitation several women who were *not* secretaries, and excluded women who *were* secretaries. To him, women were girls, and there wasn't much difference between any of them.

Ann made her invitation calls: "It's Secretaries' Day and Mr. Talcott wants to take us *all* to lunch." As she vocally underlined *all,* the recipients understood the message of his grand gesture.

When Ann's calls were completed, she thought again of the two secretaries who were not on the invitation list. Kiona was Sheila's secretary; Lisa worked for the CFO. "Maybe I'd better talk to them myself," she decided.

Ann went to look for the two women at break time in the cafeteria rather than take a chance they'd hear about the invitation from somebody else. But word of the lunch had already reached them.

"Don't feel bad, Ann," Kiona replied in her maddeningly quiet way. "I'm very pleased not to be included. That man…" Kiona could never bring herself to speak ill of anyone, not even the Bleeper.

Lisa was less understanding. "You'd think he would invite the secretaries, not the whole office," she said. She liked being treated to lunch, no matter who she had to put up with. She didn't like to eat alone, never went to lunch or coffee break by herself.

"Come on, Lisa," Ann smiled gently, "you know Mr. Talcott. He thinks all women are secretaries. He isn't leaving you out, he just doesn't see you."

"He sees me all right at five o'clock when he needs something extra typed," Lisa replied. "Okay, Kio, let's have lunch someplace special today — just us. We'll have a glass of wine, a long, leisurely lunch, and treat *ourselves* to Secretaries' Day."

"You know we can't have wine," Kiona shot back. They chimed in together, "against the rules!"

"All right, but we can have a special lunch somewhere."

"Sounds good, but let's make it eleven-thirty so we can take the extra time. He'll be busy with *them* and won't notice how long we're gone."

Ann returned to her desk, assured that feelings weren't too badly bruised among the uninvited.

THE PLEASURE OF HIS COMPANY

"Nice choice for lunch, Ann," said Jessica. "Did you tell him noon?" The seven women sat at a large round table and surveyed the ornate dining room with soft music playing in the background. The green Pacific Lounge insignia glittered on the crystal glassware and white china bread plates.

"Of course, Jess," Ann answered, looking at the vacant chair, then her watch. "It's only ten past. You know how the boss likes to make an entrance."

She had barely said the words before the women heard the commotion as their boss approached.

"Ah, there are my girls," Talcott greeted the women across the uncrowded room. The few diners in the place looked up from quiet conversations to watch the large man stride toward his table, greet his guests magnanimously like an eastern potentate, then sit down in the empty chair. Donna had drawn the seat to his right; Jessica sat to his left. Talcott pulled a starched green napkin from beneath his salad plate and took a bite of spinach leaves. The women who had waited for him to arrive did the same.

"Well now, my wife is going to sizzle when I tell her I've had lunch with seven beautiful girls," he chuckled. "Gotta tell you the one I just heard. How many broads does it take to screw in a light bulb?" He paused for a moment, then added, "None. Broads don't screw light bulbs." He waited for the laughter, which didn't come. Instead, the women leaned over their plates and pretended to be eating. Only Ann looked up with a glazed half-smile. Sheila was struggling with a full mouth and let out a choking sound. "Just heard that this morning," the boss went on. "Well, we're not here to tell jokes. This Secretaries' Day is really serious business."

The bank president swallowed another bite of salad as he rose ceremoniously and lifted his water glass. "You can't know how much I thank you for coming together today." He paused to take a sip of water. "The work you gals do for the bank really makes a difference. I know there aren't many banks that give girls the opportunity to work in management, but we at Stateside pride ourselves in having you ladies at all levels of our staff." He tipped his glass toward Sheila who nodded back at him.

"We're here on Secretaries' Day to express the bank's appreciation for your work, from the Secretary of the bank (he waved his glass at Donna) to my own special Girl Friday (nod to Ann)." You're all real gems. I only wish I could spend more time with you today. Unfortunately, I have another pressing matter. It's not all roses being head of a bank." He took a deep drink of his water, placed the glass back on the table, and then he was gone.

"Gee, aren't we thrilled he spared us those few glorious moments." Jessica spoke quietly in mock awe after she was sure he was out of earshot. "At least we got a free lunch. He *did* take the check, didn't he?"

"Come on, Jess, give him a little credit," Sheila cut in. "The guy is trying to do the right thing."

"Why couldn't he just send flowers?"

"What was that joke all about?" Judy asked. "Imagine thinking that was funny!"

"That was no joke; that was my boss," Terri waggled her fingers near her mouth, imitating Groucho Marx.

The server removed the salad plates and brought their lunches as they talked. Noticing the vacant chair, she whispered to Donna, "Will he be back?"

"No, he's gone," Donna whispered back loudly. "But bring his lunch in a doggy bag." She turned to Jessica and winked. "We can split it tomorrow."

"He really thinks he's doing us a favor when he does things like this," Ann explained. "He isn't the chauvinist you think he is. Just the other day he told me that with a woman on the Supreme Court we ought to be thinking about putting a woman on the Board of Directors."

"I don't believe it," Terri spoke up. "The day that happens we'll all be too old to watch."

"No, Terri. I've heard him say that too," Sheila leaned forward. "He really would like to have a woman on the Board, but he says the other members wouldn't stand for it."

"Do you believe that, Sheila?" Terri asked.

"No, but it sounds good, doesn't it? I guess I'd like to believe it."

Donna put down her fork. "I really don't see what difference that would make."

"If you have to ask…" Terri murmured.

"It's the idea, Donna," Jessica answered. "The idea of having a woman in a decision-making position. He'd never put up with that. Look how he runs our lives, controls our choices, even intrudes on our personal lives, and nobody complains — at least not loudly nor where he can hear.

"Ann, he calls you at home at all hours. Donna, you too. And you, Sheila, from what you've said he calls you anytime between midnight and five a.m. without even thinking."

"Well, that's part of my job," Sheila answered. "I've been around so long, he thinks of me as one of the family. We go back a lot of years. I was here when his dad was the boss, and that's a long time ago." Her eyes closed as she returned to the "good old days" for a moment.

"Hell, we're supposed to be professionals," Jessica went on, "not robots he can control whenever the hell he feels like it. Who's had a Saturday off lately? And does anyone here get paid extra for Saturdays? Donna, you even worked last Sunday, didn't you, getting ready for the quarterly report?"

"Yes, but I had to get the thing out before…"

"You see? He has us working our tails off." Jessica's voice grew more intense. "He even controls our clothes. He has us dress alike, but not the men. He wouldn't dare tell his mortgage men what to wear! Sometimes I could just scream at the way he tells us all how to do our jobs. And today, the way he rounded us all together, all his little 'secretaries'…"

"Easy," Ann said quietly. "Some of us *are* secretaries, and we like it."

"I know, Ann, that's not what I mean. According to him, if we're women we must be secretaries — he doesn't see us for what we do or who we are. We're *just women,* actually *girls.* I don't like that kind of thinking; it dilutes any authority we could ever build up. It ruins our self esteem." Jessica was venting some of the feelings left over from the annual meeting. "We are quite powerless, you know."

"What do you mean, powerless?" asked Sheila. "As a Vice President, I feel I have the authority over my department. I have... *power*, if that's what you choose to call it."

"Do you really?" asked Jessica, "or does he let you think you have power by giving you a title? What happens when he wants to counter your orders? What happens if he disagrees with your recommendations? I've seen him turn whole programs of yours clear around just because... well, just because."

"Just because what?" Sheila asked. "Just because he didn't think of it himself? Was that what you were going to say? Well, I respect his opinions and if he doesn't think something will work, who am I to question his..."

"Authority," Jessica triumphantly made her point. She looked around to see if she was drawing attention. "Now do you see what I mean?" she asked more quietly.

"But that's not power, Jess," said Judy. "Power is knowing the right answers to the right questions, knowing the right program to introduce."

Terri cut in, "I don't think so. Power is too elusive to put one meaning to it. Power has to do with moving people around where you want them, getting them to do what you want them to... like working Saturdays whether they complain or not." She grinned at Jessica.

"Okay, Terri, but to do that you need to be in a position of authority. Power is holding all the cards and being able to play them whenever *you* want. And men know how to do that; women don't. Women are always looking out for the other person's feelings."

"Perhaps, but men know how to do this because they've been at it longer and know what they're doing. I can trust them," Sheila said.

"Sure, but it's because they're on the top of the heap and know how to stay there by keeping women off the heap altogether." Jessica's voice rose again.

"You seem to think that power is some kind of game, Jessica." Ann tried to calm her friend. "If it is, why couldn't women learn to play too?"

"Sure, Jess, like that women's bank in Seattle. Why couldn't we start our own bank? We could be our own managers." Terri smiled as she made up the suggestion on the spot.

Jessica glared at them all. "I know you're playing with me. I don't think you know how much power you already have, if only you knew how to use it."

"Yes, I know how much power women *could* have, Jess." Terri still grinned. She was beginning to see Jessica's point.

"Do you remember *Alice Doesn't Day* a couple years ago?" asked Jessica. "Have you heard about it?"

Eyes widened around the table, as some vaguely recalled the non-event that could have been. "I don't remember," Terri went on, "but I read about it. NOW wanted all the working women of the country to stay home and not do any work for one whole day — including housewives. Could you imagine what would happen if women ever really did that? Tellers, secretaries, clerks, nurses, teachers, mothers, housekeepers…"

"Waitresses, farmhands, factory workers, airline attendants," from Jessica.

"…could you ever dream of such a gigantic shut down? Apparently they couldn't… or at least they didn't. They were afraid of losing their jobs. A few Alices picketed; a few wore armbands…"

"I did my usual work," Jessica went on, "but I couldn't afford to risk my job. It was a new one. So I wore my armband and I typed, as usual, but I added a note to every letter I typed. The notes read: *If this woman wasn't working here today, this letter would not have been typed. Happy* Alice Doesn't Day."

"What happened?" Judy asked.

"What's NOW?" Winnie added.

"NOW is the National Organization for Women, big stuff in the '70s." Sheila remembered it well. "That walkout was for just a few hours, in Atlanta, near where I lived. I don't recall that it resulted in much. The male media poo-poohed it, saying it didn't faze business at all."

Before Sheila could continue, Jessica answered Judy. "Not much happened; Sheila's right. The other women in the office thought I was flirting with disaster, that I was terribly bold and wicked. The men just smiled and threw the notes in the wastebasket."

"Just think," Terri continued dreamily, "if it had worked! Perhaps Mr. Jefferson was right — a little rebellion is good."

The women around the table in the midst of the now-busy restaurant became silent for a few moments.

Then, softly, "Wouldn't that be something? All our tellers away from their windows for just one day. Bleeper wouldn't be able to stay open; there aren't enough men in the bank who know how to operate the teller machines." Winnie smiled as she looked off in the distance. "Just think of the impact. You know, there *is* a lot of power in those teller cages." She emphasized the word *cages*.

"They'd be afraid of losing their jobs," Donna offered. "And they wouldn't jeopardize those pitiful little paychecks."

"No," Sheila countered. "I don't think they would refuse to go along just because of their paychecks. I agree they wouldn't cooperate, but for a different reason. I don't think they would let their customers go without service. Those are dedicated girls... er, women," she glanced at Jessica who smiled to acknowledge the correction. "They wouldn't let their customers down."

"You can say that, Sheila, because that's what you would tell them... as their boss, that is. You'd lay it on thick about 'customer service'. But if you were a teller on that line and looking for a way to show how important your job is, wouldn't you walk out, even for just one day?"

"Certainly not... no," she raised her voice defensively. "Our customers are mostly women, and I don't think they would understand what was going on."

"Then you think power is numbers," said Jessica.

"No, I don't," Sheila answered.

"Of course not," Jessica was jubilant. "If it were, women would have it, wouldn't they? There are more of us."

"Power is being on top, and being on top is having superior knowledge." This from Judy. "Those who get the best education are the ones in power. Those who know most about the business are in power. It's always been that way. Knowledge is power."

"Oh really," Winnie smiled with her sexy look and lowered her voice demurely. "I always thought men found something *else* powerful in women."

"Come on, Winnie, be serious," Jessica cautioned, then added thoughtfully, "or are you?" Winnie was having a bad enough time with her latest broken relationship, but would she really consider sex as a tool to gain power over men?

Winnie continued in mock seriousness, "All right, let's lay out a plan to put some women in power at Stateside. You know, another vice president, or president, or member of the Board… or something."

"Sure, and how long would our jobs last when the Bleeper heard about it?" asked Donna.

"Hank would kill me if I lost this paycheck," Judy added.

"Okay," Winnie went on, "we could start an underground movement that would get a woman elected at the next annual meeting and let her take over from there." She was enjoying the idea of subterfuge.

"Kinda like the CIA," Terri joined in the fun. "We could call ourselves: Chicks In Action, you know, CIA, and put a woman up for director and all turn up at next year's shareholders meeting and vote her in."

"Sorry, ladies," said the Corporate Secretary. "Elections are all determined ahead of time, you know that. The votes are cast by proxy, so I'm afraid your little scheme wouldn't have a chance."

"Cold Water Donna," teased Terri and continued undaunted. "Maybe we ought to form our own proxy group. We would have the vote and the power to put a woman where she belongs."

"You know Terri, that's not a half-bad idea." Jessica was taking more interest in the direction this conversation was taking. "That might not be too far off."

"It's a screwy piece of nonsense and you know it, Jessica," Sheila said as she was getting ready to leave. "Mr. Talcott would never let you get started on a move like that."

"Maybe he wouldn't have to know. Maybe we could go underground, as Terri says."

"Yeah, CIA... or even PLO, Proxy Liberation Organization," added Terri, who had been doodling with acronyms as they talked.

The women's voices dropped, their faces turned serious. The moment slowed noticeably. Then Jessica began, "Maybe... we... could." Silence as each woman followed her own thoughts. "Maybe... by some outside chance... maybe... we could gather enough votes to swing the next election... maybe..."

"Sure! We could set up our own proxy committee." It was Terri's suggestion. "Then we could get all the tellers to ask customers for new signatures. Jess could collect them and Donna could change the script for the meeting. It might be worth the try."

"Maybe we could," Jessica was still thinking. "We could print up new proxy cards naming a new committee to cast votes, send them to the customers we know and ask the tellers to give them to customers they know. We could have cards mailed back... no, we'll need a post office box where we can pick them up periodically. Maybe we can get enough votes to offset the other proxy committee. That's what it's all about, isn't it? Outnumbering the other committee? What do you think?"

"I think it's the silliest idea I've ever heard." Sheila stood up and put on her coat. "Such a silly idea would never get past Mr. Talcott."

"I think it's a super idea, worth the try," answered Terri, always looking for excitement, especially concerning the empowerment of women.

"You're out of your minds," Sheila scoffed.

"It might work," said Donna, "but why would we want to do it?"

"Because it is something that has to be done," Winnie said. "We have to show the tellers the kind of power they have being 'on the line' next to the customers and money."

"Winnie, you've tried bringing in labor leaders before to look at a union, and it didn't work. The tellers were scared," Terri pointed out.

"Somehow, we have to show the tellers their worth, while we show those old men in the Board Room that they need the women at the teller windows."

"At the same time we can let them know that a woman in the Board Room might improve the entire business," Donna added.

"Judy, what do you think?"

"It might work. But we have to realize we all could lose our jobs, if not our necks, if it doesn't. Frankly, I'm a little scared of what you are talking about, and a lot scared of what we are thinking. Maybe we ought to do some research, ask a few questions, find out just how much risk we're letting ourselves in for. There may be some major flaw in your plan that we haven't considered."

"Sheila?" Jessica looked at the ranking bank officer in the group as she stood glaring at her co-workers. "What do you think?"

"I don't like it. I don't think it has a chance. I prefer not to take part, but I…" she was thinking fast, "…I won't blow the whistle either. Go ahead as Judy suggests and get more input before you jump to a decision. But whatever you do, leave me out. I know nothing. I have worked damn hard to get where I am, and I don't want to lose my spot on the ladder, no matter how loose you think the rung might be." Sheila turned and strode out of the restaurant.

"Okay," Jessica began, "we'll get some information together, consider the risks, and focus on all the power at the teller windows. We can think of a plan — it'll be something to do. How about getting together again in a couple weeks? Donna, can you check on proxy laws by then?"

"Sure. Isn't your birthday coming up, Winnie?"

"Yes, a week from Wednesday."

"Okay, let's go to lunch again that day and compare notes. I'll look up the proxy laws and let you know what rules we have to follow." Donna already had discounted the plan. She knew the risks. Maybe the facts would discourage the others — at least keep them out of jail.

The server refilled coffee cups a last time for the women of the Stateside Bank Secretaries' Day celebration. She watched them lift their cups in a silent toast, smiling among themselves, like a ritual closing of some kind of secret meeting. She caught their whispered words, "Power to the Proxies", as she placed the check in the middle of the table.

Thank you, AT&T

Jessica didn't scream on the trip home the evening after the *Secretaries' Day* luncheon. She had too much to think about. When she walked into the kitchen, her head was still whirling with possibilities.

"Hi, kiddos," she called cheerily as she headed for her room to kick off her shoes and change clothes.

"She's in a good mood," Richard noted to Amy. "Hey, Mom, I'm going over to Jerry's to work on his computer. Okay?" Hearing the echo of his okay, Richard grabbed his jacket and left.

Amy called to her mother, "Are you ready for something delicious?"

"Sure am, sweetie," responded Jessica, pulling her sweatshirt over her head as she entered the kitchen.

"How was your day?" Amy asked dutifully, but the ringing phone interrupted.

"Hi, Dan," Jess smiled into the phone. "How's Chicago?"

"Unusually warm for spring," Dan returned. "How's the weather out there?"

She answered cautiously, suspecting he was sizing up things for a visit. "Rainy, as usual, although the temperature is moving up a bit. At least it's semi-warm rain. Any special reason for checking the weather?"

"Jess, I'm planning my summer vacation. Schedules have to be re-worked and all that. Would you and the kids be up for renting a cottage on the Peninsula and taking a vacation together with me and my kids?" He shot out the question then held his breath.

"Well… ah… wow… what an idea." She was trying to come up with an answer that wasn't a commitment. "Where'd that come from? Summer is still a long way off."

"It seems I get the children for four weeks and I know they'd be bored to tears in my apartment here for all that time. Besides, I think it's time your kids and mine met each other. How about it?"

"Dan, oh Dan, it sounds good. But think about it. Your kids won't be happy with me there. They may even hate my kids just because they're mine…"

"I wouldn't," Amy cut in. "I'd like to meet his kids. I could handle that. And Richard would too. I just know he would."

"Hear that? You have a rooting section here. Amy thinks it would be keen. Richard is out right now."

"Jess, give it some thought. Talk to Richard and see what you can come up with. We could get away with a three-room cottage. My three can share a room, yours too, and we could have the third. How about it? Come on, say yes."

"It might be better for the boys to share a room and the girls to have their own room." Good god, she was actually planning this. "Well, we'll see. When are you scheduling this getaway? I'll have to put in for time off too. I may be able to manage only two weeks, though."

"Let's try for the last week of June and the Fourth of July."

"Sounds good. I'll check it out with Personnel tomorrow."

"Love you, Jess. I hope we can work this out. It'll be a big step for us."

"Yeah, me too."

"Goodnight."

"Goodnight, Dan."

"No mushy stuff?" asked Amy when Jess had hung up the phone.

"Nah, we save that for when the kids are in bed."

"Nice try, Mom. But I'm not a kid anymore."

"Oh really? Ten years old and not a kid. What are you then?"

"I'll be a pre-teen in a couple of months. That's moving up, isn't it?"

"Sure. That's moving up," smiled Jessica as she hugged her growing-up daughter.

Later that night, as Jessica lay waiting for sleep to come, she went over the events of the day — the luncheon that laid the groundwork for some pretty heavy dreams. *What if? What if? What if? Should I be thinking about a plan that might threaten my job? Might I be tempted to marry Dan just because I was to lose my job? Would the children suffer if I wasn't bringing home the bacon?* Her thoughts were turning into sleepy dreams when the telephone rang, abruptly cutting off more questions. She automatically grabbed it before it could ring twice and spoke, "Jessica here," as she did at the office.

"Hi, Jessica Here. How are you?"

The voice was unmistakable. Besides, only Will called that late. Jess didn't turned on the light.

"Hi yourself. I'm fine, just great. What about you?"

"I'm missing you. Missing you more than I'd like. How I wish you were in my arms at this very moment."

"Yeah, wouldn't that be nice?" Jessica knew she sounded skeptical, but she didn't think Will would hear it.

"Jessie?" Only Will could get away with that nickname.

"Yes, Will."

"Jessie, I have to see you — soon. I have to hold you — soon. I need to have you by my side. How about if I fly up next week? Can you get away for a day or so?"

"Not during the week. No. I can't get away during the week. And next weekend is bad too." A long pause indicated that Will wasn't pleased with the response. "But I might be able to get away one night. You'd probably have some business during the day anyway. I could join you for dinner and…"

"Well, if that's the best you can do. Maybe after I get you in my arms I can convince you to stay there. I'll fly in sometime Wednesday and stay until Friday. Can you make reservations for me… us?"

"Usual place?"

"Sure. Usual place." Another long pause, then, "I really miss you, darling. I may have some news for you by next Wednesday."

"Oh really? What kind of news?"

"Maybe I shouldn't have said anything. But, we'll talk about it when I get there. See you Wednesday."

"Okay, but not even a hint?"

"No. Not until I have you in my arms. I love you so, Jessie."

"Yeah. Me too." Somehow, Jessica had a great deal of trouble saying the words I-love-you. Maybe it was because she didn't quite believe them coming from Will. He had said them so often, had made so many promises, had broken so many of them. Jessica was never sure when to believe him, when to hope, and when to discount him. So she covered herself by discounting most of what he said. Actions speak louder than words, she repeatedly told herself.

She replaced the phone receiver carefully, turned over and closed her eyes. Dan. Will. Will. Dan. I don't say *I love you* to either one of them. Is it because I'm not sure if I do? Can a woman love two men? Should she cast her lot with either of them? If so, which one?

"Too much to think about," she said aloud. "Let's get back to the important stuff. A proxy takeover. Now there is something to think about." Recalling the plans discussed at luncheon, she drifted off blissfully to sleep.

Donna – The Game Plan

Donna Westerhoff, Stateside's Corporate Secretary, looked right at home searching company records and administrative files. The corporate officer with a law degree looked equally at home in the university's law library. She spent lunch hours and odd moments at both places for most of the next week. Nothing she found indicated the women were treading on dangerous ground, at least not legally dangerous. On the contrary, she discovered the free enterprise system is weighted on the side of the shareholder and therefore on rights by proxy.

Holding the latest copy of "Administrative Proxy Regulations" in her lap, she looked at the law students studying at desks around the room. She had been one of them once, ten… no twelve years ago. Somehow she had known then that she lacked the fierce competitiveness that kept these budding lawyers at their grueling studies.

Law students, she found, are strange and somber people, lacking the threads of humor that Donna counted on to keep her alive. There was a do-or-die aura that enshrouded these young people, and Donna knew early in law school she wanted nothing to do with the competitive atmosphere of law practice. She stuck it out, but after graduation refused to even think about taking bar examinations. She didn't want to risk losing her light-hearted spirit in the quest for official lawyerhood. She would use her legal knowledge in ways other than as a practicing attorney, working in the field of law without giving up her own luster.

Sometimes though, like now, she admired the desires that fueled the great need to strive for excellence in this field. All these young people seemed to have it. Poor things!

"You just aren't a competitor," her Legal Procedures prof had pointed out to her. "You lack that spirit that keeps these kids fighting to stay in school."

"If I have to kick and scratch to stay and study law, then I'll go somewhere else, do something else," she had told him. She stayed, deciding that finishing law school was important enough to *fight* for.

Now in her mid-forties, facing another cause, another opportunity to use competition to get something she thought important, Donna had misgivings. Was the cause of putting a woman in the Board Room important enough to use war tactics on co-workers? She couldn't say it was. Yet, she hadn't decided it wasn't. Was anything that important?

Donna had always been content to stay near power, shielding herself from it directly. As a young bride she had stood next to her husband who coached winning college football teams. His power led a bunch of scruffy players to the top of the heap, providing the respect that encompassed them and provided her with the feeling of being near power. The college regents had been very grateful for those winning teams.

All her life Donna had experienced the power of her father, a police captain. To her, power was incorporated in a uniform, a position, a man. She believed that nothing she could do would be enough to give her the power to rival the men in her life. The next best thing was to be next to power, daughter of a cop, wife of a powerful coach, worker in the office next to an influential bank president, basking in the power that went with *their* positions.

"Actually, I don't really need power for myself," she once had told Jessica. "I guess I was born deficient, but I'll leave the power grabbing to others."

Yet, here she was, researching ways to move the power of the bank customers into the hands of a few women. "That might not be too bad an idea," she allowed herself to think for the first time. "After all, there is justice in giving credit to the women who do all the work — the tellers. I know Mr. Talcott couldn't take care of a single customer transaction; he doesn't know how. Maybe it's only right to provide representation for all those working people at the bottom of the heap." She breathed deeply at the significance of that thought passing unchallenged through her head.

Donna produced the results of her research the following Wednesday at the luncheon meeting to celebrate Winnie's birthday. After the women had placed their orders, they sat back, overtly surveyed the room for "spies", then turned to Donna.

"All I could find was the general regulation stating that the latest date on the proxy card is what counts. The card has to designate the voting proxy; it must be signed, and it must be dated. That's the meat."

"Great," was Jessica's response, an excitement in her voice as she began to think aloud. "We need a plan, some security, some dates, and a budget."

"A budget?" asked Judy. "What do you mean, budget? How much is this going to cost us anyway?" Judy, always broke, reacted in panic to any mention of money.

"Don't worry, Judy," Jessica reassured her. "We'll work out the costs and pool our bonuses if we have to. Won't we? What do you all think?"

"If it doesn't cost too much," Winnie offered. "How much are you thinking about? I mean, what expenses could there be?"

"First, printing costs. We'll need some new proxy cards. I know a woman printer who will do the job for us, give us a price break and keep her mouth shut. The other big expense will be postage. We'll need to send a mailing to most customers to get their proxies. And we'll need a new Proxy Committee. That won't cost money, but I just thought of it, and we'd better take care of it now. We can take the new cards with us whenever any of us visits a branch office — and pick up signed ones to return."

Terri cut in, "Hey, I've got an idea. Let's use code words like the guys do… you know, sports terms and stuff like that. Then we can play this game at their level, use their strategies and talk their talk… except it will be ours and they won't understand."

"What do you mean?" asked Donna.

"You know, like instead of calling them *proxy cards*, we can call them 'tickets'. And *tellers* can be 'players', and *customers* can be 'boosters', and a packet of signed 'tickets' can be a 'touchdown' or something."

"Not bad," said Jessica. "We'll work on that. Right now we need a Proxy Committee, er… *Coaching Staff*. How's that, Terri?"

"Oooh," moaned the others. But Jessica continued. "I'll volunteer. How about you, Winnie and Judy?"

"No, I couldn't," answered Judy. "I… uh… I'd rather not."

Jessica wouldn't press. "Okay, how about you, Donna?"

"Well, if you think I should," Donna responded. "Although I'd rather coach from the sidelines. Is that okay for coded language? Hey, I've had experience, at least in football and police talk."

"Yeah, I think you should," Jessica went on. "In fact, I think all our names should be on that proxy committee. Let's think about that one. We have time to decide later. I just thought of a code name for the whole action. How about using the name 'Alice'?"

"Like 'Alice Doesn't Day'? Or do you mean like the movie 'Alice Doesn't Live Here Anymore'?" Terri asked.

"Both! Of course, only this time Alice Does! Better yet, make it Alices, plural, all of us! The Alices Proxy Committee."

As soon as the name was decided and the committee selected, the plans began to fall into place. Jessica kept a notebook with dates and schedules. The tellers would be brought in one at a time, making absolutely sure of their support for the plan before exposing details. They would require a pledge of cooperation and of silence about the Alices.

Jessica continued explaining the operation; the group could see she had thought it all out. "All new account holders will receive a new proxy card to sign, dated currently. Donna will handle the big accounts, the ones with multiple votes, making certain the accounts are all named on the cards. Every account holder is allowed one vote for each $100 on deposit. In addition, each mortgagee has one vote. So the bulk of the voting power is where the money is."

"Isn't it always?" Winnie commented dryly.

The women decided that cards with cover letters would be mailed to customers with large accounts at the same time as the pre-Christmas marketing mailer. That way they could piggy-back on a regular mailing and save some postage. They also decided the majority of the cards would have to be in their files by Thanksgiving, just before the mailing. There was a lot of work to do in the months until then.

"We can do it." Terri was confident. "All it takes is to keep our guards up and our eyes open. Nearly half our customers come into the branch offices at least once a month," she said. "That gives us two or three months to get more than half our customers. The mailing will take care of the rest. But we have to be sure to get one of *us* assigned to do that mailing."

Sheila had been silently listening to all the plans, saying nothing more than "Pass the butter." Now, however, she had to speak. "Wait a minute, you're getting into my territory now. I can't let you use the pre-Christmas mailing for your purposes. I said I wouldn't blow the whistle, but you're sitting in my backyard, and this thing could blow up in *my* face."

Jessica turned and spoke sharply. "Sheila, don't you realize that your job is just as much at risk as any of ours if we don't get some women representation at the top? Can't you see that no matter how long you've been with the company, how loyal you are, and how much you think Talcott trusts you and needs you, he'd get rid of you tomorrow if he thought it would save a buck. If someone came along who would work like you do and ask for a smaller salary…?" She left the idea unfinished.

"I don't think so, Jessica. I've been around here too long to get a raw deal like that. Besides, I'm good at my job and I do it without giving Mr. Talcott more problems. He couldn't get along without me." Hearing how strange that sounded spoken aloud, she added, "at least not well." She chuckled, but she didn't feel like laughing. Deep down, she knew what Jessica said was close to the truth. If it suited his purpose, Talcott would move her to a teller window or worse, out the door. She knew it, but she didn't want to know it.

"What about a mailing address, Jessica?" Judy broke the awkward silence. "We can't have Alice's mail coming to the office. Where will the new proxies… er, tickets… be mailed?"

"Good question," Jessica remarked. "I'll use my post office box. Better yet, I'll rent a new box for the occasion. Then it won't be traceable, even if the wrong people should get their hands on a card. But we'll have to be darned careful that doesn't happen."

"It all sounds so, so subversive," said Donna. "Let's hear it all from the top, the game plan, I mean. Go over it again, and start with the goal and objectives. Just so we all know where we're going and how."

"Here goes." Jessica read from her notes. "Our goal is to represent women on the Board of Directors and top management." She looked up and added, "something that the Boss has fought against for ages." She continued to read: "Our objective is to elect a woman member to the Board of Directors. Our strategy is to control the proxy votes at the annual shareholders' meeting next January. We'll get a list of all shareholders and the size of their accounts from a computer printout and begin to acquire new proxies. My printer friend will be sworn to secrecy when I promise her more work as we get a foothold in the company, and the cards will be moved into the branches very slowly and very carefully.

"You people in Customer Service," she looked at Winnie, "will make personal contact with larger accounts, feel them out for loyalty, gain their confidence, and obtain new proxies. If it appears they are close friends of the Bleeper, forget it. A few votes won't matter. We're looking for a broad base.

"Then we'll use the holiday mailing for the last big push." She looked straight at Sheila. "Isn't that the time the Talcotts go on their southern cruise vacation, Donna?"

"Yes, right after Thanksgiving. He'll be gone about three weeks."

"Well, that might make it easier, but not completely safe. We'll have to send a letter of explanation in the mailing and make sure people send the proxies to the post office box rather than bring them in. And we'll only have those few days to do it.

"The final step will be collecting all the proxies, carrying them to the annual meeting and placing them at the feet of those old men and declaring a majority of the votes." Jessica paused for the effect — that marvelous moment they were all working toward.

"But what if he finds out?" Sheila asked the dreaded question that hovered in the back of everyone's mind.

"If he finds out," Jessica stopped. "If he finds out... he does. That's all. Let's just hope it is too late, or that he doesn't find out at all. I'm certainly not going to tell him." She looked directly at Sheila and the older woman heard the message.

"No, Jessica, I'm not going to tell him either. I wish you luck, but I don't believe you can pull it off."

"We'll see."

Then in the midst of the sedate restaurant, soothed by a background of quiet piped-in music, luncheon guests were stunned to see a table of women suddenly stand, thrust their hands to the center of the table forming a large, massive fist, shake hands together, and shout, "The Alices are on their way!"

Then followed a chorus of "Happy Birthday, Winnie."

ADDENDUM:

The proxy card is very simple. It carries the shareholder's name and account number at the top and it reads as follows:

REVOCABLE PROXY AGREEMENT

WHEREAS, This Bank functions through its officers and it is desirable to have all members or a large percentage of them present at annual and special meetings or to have them properly represented so that the Bank will be in a position to act,

THEREFORE, in consideration of the ownership of a share in STATESIDE SAVINGS BANK, Capital City, and the desire of the undersigned to be represented at meetings of members of said Bank, the undersigned hereby appoints:

> PROXY COMMITTEE, as duly constituted by, and operating under rules of the Board of Directors of said Bank

as proxy to vote and act for the undersigned at any regular or special meeting of the members of said Bank at which the undersigned is not personally present, and the undersigned expressly authorizes said proxy to appoint a substitute with full power to vote and act at such meetings in the absence of said proxy.

It is understood that the undersigned will vote in person when present and that this proxy may be revoked at any time in writing by notice to the Bank, but this proxy shall remain in force from year to year until revoked in writing.

Dated and Signed.

The Alices Committee changed the indented paragraph to read:
> PROXY OPERATIONS GROUP
> as selected by the independent voter representatives
> holding this card.

The Alices Committee further added:

This proxy revokes any previously dated proxy and supersedes other signed proxies.

THE MEN IN HER LIFE
(BESIDES DAN)

Jessica's love life was not simple. Before her marriage, she had worked at a Seattle TV station, where she had a brief but emotionally charged affair with Will, one of the executives. By the time she learned he was married, it didn't matter. She was sure they loved each other in a soul-mate kind of relationship. Then Will's mother-in-law saw them together in a place they shouldn't be, and the affair was over — at least for a while.

Will moved his family to Los Angeles, ostensibly to start over, and Jessica poured her wounded heart into her work.

Phil

Phil Nadeau came along at just the right time to rescue Jessica from a thwarted love. She fell hard for the handsome police officer while she was interviewing him for a story. They were married a year later, just before Richard was born. Jess forgot about Will in her excitement at becoming a wife and mother all at once.

Jessica and Phil had an idyllic marriage for their time. These flower children had grown up into parenthood and were learning the responsibilities of adult living. They were trying to put back a world that had fallen apart during riots, assassinations, political intrigue, and treachery. Believing they were succeeding, they brought Amy into the world four years later.

That world shattered for Jessica just before Amy's first birthday when Phil was killed during a high-speed chase in his patrol car. Jess bravely assumed full responsibility for her children. She was thirty-four, healthy, educated. However, the early '80s was not the time to be looking for a cushy job.

After Phil died, Jessica devoted all her energies to making a life for her children. Phil's insurance helped her through a couple years at a low-paying ad agency job. But she knew she had to do more. She wanted to do more. That's when Jessica looked toward developing a career with Stateside Savings Bank.

Will

Jess's heart remained tied to Will Barton. So when he chose to walk back into Jessica's life after a few years, he was still married. How often had he told her he was getting a divorce? Theirs had been one of those *magical* romances that budded, flowered, and was lost within a few short months. Theirs, Jess realized later, was the typical married-man-single-woman affair that would never go anywhere. Still, he kept popping up at odd moments, kept insisting their love was as star-crossed and forever as it had seemed at first. And Jess turned into a marshmallow whenever he called.

One moment she would be the reasonable, rational businesswoman in complete control of her life. The next, the phone would ring and she would turn to mush. Irrational? Certainly. Unreasonable? Definitely. She knew it, but she still turned to mush.

After Dan entered her on-off romantic life, she talked to Donna about her affair with Will. Without using his name, she tried to explain, "I just melt when he takes my hand or puts his arm around me."

But Donna misunderstood, remarking, "Phil was a knight in police academy armor, if I ever saw one. And you're right not to forget him, but you have to move on with your life. This new fellow, Dan, the one who makes you melt. Give him a chance. If he's the right one, you'll know. If he isn't, you'll know that too."

In her heart, Jessica already knew. Away from Will, she dated, played the field for a time, occasionally abandoning her good taste to get back in the game. She managed to find a few male friends, but no one who interested her romantically until Dan came along.

The Bleeper

His full name was Thomas J. Talcott Jr. He had dropped the Junior after his father died. The staff called him the *Bleeper*, a kind of code name they used as a warning when he made his unscheduled visits to their offices. Because everyone knew that Talcott disapproved of smoking, coffee drinking, swearing, and women in business, his visits were preceded with a kind of bleeper warning. Ash trays and coffee cups disappeared, tongues were put on good behavior, and women tried to fade into the background.

He was an old man, maybe in his late sixties, overweight (obviously he didn't disapprove of food), and he wheezed as he made his rounds, office to office, inspecting. At his approach, whispers swept the office, "The Bleeper is on the way; the Bleeper is in the parking lot; the Bleeper is in the teller area; the Bleeper is moving toward the Accounting Department." Backs straightened. Even the customers felt the electricity of the impending visit, knowing that something special was taking place.

Jessica remembered the first time she saw him during one of those inspections. While she had been briefed, the reality of this power figure still amazed her. She was on the phone when she became aware of his entrance. He stood at the door, dictating a message into the small recorder held by a vice president. Clearly, he was assessing and rating the general appearance of the office, placing on record his first impressions, and noting in detail any infraction of rules. There were so many rules, it is no wonder the Bleeper didn't trust his memory and insisted upon recording everything.

The Bleeper *appeared* to remember names, although he probably didn't. He breezed through the office calling out jovially, "Hi, Adams; hello Smith; nice job, Hanson." Likely he was briefed at the door by his veep. He always addressed the men, but never the women. Which probably was because most of the management were men — chief loan officers were men, and all the vice presidents — except Sheila McDowell, a long-time family friend.

That day six years ago, Jessica remembered, she had stayed on the phone long after her caller had hung up. She endured the monotone buzz in her ear in order to appear occupied while the old man made his inspection, made friendly gestures to the men, and moved on. It gave her an opportunity to watch, to stare in amazement, all the while appear to be working — just another woman doing her job.

Jessica didn't realize until later that what the boss was telling his recorder was, "Make a note that all branch managers are to meet me at the door when I come for inspection and accompany me during the tour."

As he moved out of the office, coffee mugs reappeared, shoulders relaxed, and women resumed their duties with the customers. Jessica, who had worked in many offices during her career, had never seen a show like the Bleeper put on. Yet, she knew it was for real.

Stories abounded about people who had been fired for having an ash try or coffee mug on their desks, or for using a cuss word in the Bleeper's presence. Once he even opened a desk drawer and, upon finding a sandwich, had fired its hungry owner on the spot. Nobody doubted he had also fired someone for drinking coffee before nine-thirty (another rule).

That morning her crew apparently passed muster. Jessica had wondered then if she would ever learn all the rules.

None of the rules were written down; she learned about the coffee her first day on the job. She had poured herself a cup of coffee upon arriving at the office, only to have it snatched from her hand. The head teller bravely told her he was saving her life. "The Bleeper, er, excuse me, the boss doesn't approve of drinking coffee, period, and allows it only as long as we don't drink it before nine-thirty. I think he believes we'll get more work done or something."

The Bleeper's beverage of choice was tea, and no one had ever tested the theory that it was okay to drink tea as he did before that magic hour: nine-thirty a.m. Jessica never took chances after that first day. She asked permission to do anything and everything, and it helped her produce a record of marketing department longevity greater than the last three directors altogether. It was a wise decision.

The Bleeper was a man of rules. He made them up as easily as someone else might break them. A tyrant, he liked to know what was going on at all times. Like the inspections. He needed to know how each department and office looked and who was there. He felt that he lost the control if he didn't make the on-site inspections regularly. He tried to get around to all twenty-nine branches at least once a quarter.

Jessica was kicked upstairs to the Marketing Department about six months after she joined the bank. She was managing the home branch at the time, enjoying the work for which she was underpaid, but happy at having any kind of job at all. In a tyrannical outburst, Talcott had fired the marketing director and instantly ordered a new one. When a quick review of personnel files showed Jessica's experience in advertising, she was offered the job.

"Think about this before you answer," was the way Sheila McDowell had approached her. Sheila did much of the boss' legwork. Since she had uncovered Jessica's talent, she was given the task of getting her to do the work for the least amount of pay.

"Working for Mr. Talcott would be a... challenge." She chose her words carefully. "No marketing director has ever lasted more than six months. If you're fired, you may be moved back here, or you may have to leave the company."

The challenge was too much for Jessica. She knew she had abilities to soothe savage beasts, and she wanted to test them with an old bear like Talcott. "I'd appreciate the opportunity, Sheila, if you think I can do the work."

"No doubt you can do the work, Jess. I just wonder if you can take the heat."

The first time Jessica sat in Talcott's office, he had warned her, "Don't mother me!" Out of nowhere, he had made it plain he didn't like anyone hovering over him — yet he liked to be waited on. "Strange man," Jessica thought at the time. And every one of the days in her seven years since had supported that observation. Every day her assessment of him was borne out by stranger and stranger actions.

The annual meeting was another way to show his power, his control. He ran the whole thing. He told Donna how to prepare the scripts: who would be assigned to make which motions, and who would second them. He choreographed the entire performance like a ballet, with no surprises, and especially without any members of the press in the room. It always looked and sounded the same.

The president, dressed in his ceremonial black suit, would breeze into the room, move grandly to the head of the cloth-draped table on the dingy stage, grab the walnut gavel and bring it down hard on the block, intoning a somber "Call the meeting to order." He then would fall into his chair and wait for the next cue.

Jessica found a fascination for working in an environment that functioned with strict rules. She didn't like them, but found the rigidity was rather like the games she used to play as a child. "Step on a crack, break your mother's back." Strong father image, for sure, she thought. But the old goat certainly lacked the qualities of being an acceptable head of the family.

In the Name of Love

When Jessica returned to her desk after lunch, the message was waiting. "He's back and he'll meet you at six for dinner." No name; no need for one. The old feelings of excitement and intrigue returned. Jessica tingled like a teenager on a first date.

Will was special. They had both known the specialness of their relationship from the beginning. It was the eyes-across-the-room meeting that stokes the romance novels. Jessica had never believed in that mushy stuff until it happened to her. When she met Will all those years ago, how many? Fifteen? No, seventeen. Actually eighteen! She was a flower child of the late '60s, just out of college, working her first job at the Seattle television station. He was so… administrative, so important in his white shirt and dark suit. She, who had dated only flower children in their polyester bell pants and flowered shirts, was impressionable — and impressed, especially by the conservative corporate world.

Will spotted her at the same moment and found her refreshing, different from the painted polished women he knew — his mother, his older sister, his aunts, his wife. Next to Jessica, they seemed like attic relics, not quite part of the picture. However great Jess's looks, it was her curious mind grasping at odds and ends that intrigued Will. No matter what subject they were discussing, she always came up with bits of information related, sometimes only distantly, to the topic. "Did you know that the majority of television sets are located in bedrooms?" "Do you realize that children watch thousands of murders on television and never one act of love?"

As in most office romances, only the couple themselves thought they were keeping secrets. Their long stares across desks and lunch tables were obvious to anyone who cared to watch. Their dinner meetings, weekend trysts, shared projects were all clearly interpreted by other staff members. Only Will and Jess and, for a time, Will's wife, didn't realize how obvious they were.

Then it was over. After about four months, it was over. No, not with the wife walking in at an inopportune time, but with Will confessing to her his affair with Jessica (after his mother-in-law threatened to do it for him). Somehow he had a confusing idea his wife would understand how smitten he was and feel joyful for him and his new love. She wasn't. She presented him simultaneously with the information that she was pregnant with their fourth child, and with the suggestion he fire Jessica.

Jess thought she understood why he chose to stay with his wife. But she had hoped the ardor Will shared with her was enough to withstand the pull of his family. They belonged together — fate, kismet, destiny. Will's daddy, part-owner in the TV station, believed otherwise. He had his own ways of convincing his errant son of the proper behavior given the situation.

And so Jessica left town, with Will still swearing his love for her as she packed and drove off. And she believed him. She took a job at a small station in Idaho. He called her a few times to promise he was asking for a divorce, that he'd leave as soon as the new baby was born, that he loved her, and needed her and…

By the time she moved back to Seattle a year later, Will and his growing little family had moved to Los Angeles, and Jessica went on with her life. Within a few months, she met Phillip Nadeau, a handsome police officer who sometimes patrolled downtown where she worked. She met him in a waterside park one lunch hour while she was eating a taco salad. They struck up a conversation that ended with marriage vows a few months later.

Will faded into the background. He came back into focus about two years after Phil's death. One day she picked up the telephone and it was like the intervening years hadn't happened. Once more she was listening, mesmerized, to Will's protestations of love and faithfulness to her. Well yes, his wife had had a fifth baby since they last met, but she didn't mean anything to him. He was just doing his fatherly thing. It was really Jessica he loved and could they get together.

Jessica in her need for romance had wanted so much to believe him that she didn't ask any more questions. She left it to Will's conscience to periodically protest for a divorce and voice his desire to marry Jessica. Since they reconnected, Will had made several trips to Seattle.

A couple times they had met in Portland and once in San Francisco for long weekends. He was still protesting and desiring that night when they met in the hotel lounge. They hugged briefly, then found a quiet corner to catch up. He sat with his arm around her and repeated all his plans. They kissed gently, and Jessica wished she could believe him.

All through dinner, she brought him up to date about her work, her career plans, leaving out all mention of the Alices plan. That was something she wouldn't share with anyone, not just yet. Jess thought Will was listening to her report; he provided appropriate uh-huhs and ohs. But when she was finished, somewhere about the cheese course, he asked how her new assistant was working out.

"Assistant? What assistant? I don't have an assistant."

"Oh! I thought you said you had a new assistant when we talked on the phone the other night."

"I don't recall talking about work to you on the phone." She brushed aside the incident until later. Several nights later. Then it struck her and she understood clearly he must have been talking to someone else, another woman-not-his-wife. He had often mentioned other women friends, but this was the first slip… no it wasn't. He had slipped before, asking her about things he thought she had said to him. She overlooked them, not wanting to admit that she might be one of many.

The remainder of that evening was hazy for Jessica, thinking back on it. Except for one thing — his attention. He seemed interested in the waiter, the decorations, the orchestra, the hotel accommodations, the view from his window, the size of the suite, the cheapness of the blankets, just about everything except Jessica. In the middle of their lovemaking, he thought of a telephone call he had to make. As she was getting into the shower the next morning, he received a call from his wife.

He offered to drive Jessica to her office and sat distractedly while she gathered her things together. All the excitement of their meeting had dissipated within the first few hours, and Jess felt like they were straining to go through the motions of being together.

Back at home, Jess entered her bedroom with a sinking feeling that she and Will were over. Something was missing. It had been a lustrous brilliant dream, but she was awake now and the dream was gone. The feeling of a huge emptiness took hold of her, and she closed her door and cried.

Nearly a week passed before Will called again. This time he called at the office and teased her when she answered, his old charm oozing through the phone. *Beware, Jessica,* she warned herself.

But she couldn't remain nonchalant when Will said simply, "My marriage is over. We're getting a divorce. I love you. I'll call you." That was all.

The follow-up call had failed to materialize over the next several days. Jess thought surely he would call with details. But she heard nothing. After two long weeks, the old uncertainties returned to fill a restless, sleepless night. As she lay waiting for some kind of drowsiness, she thought, *why can't I handle men more like Winnie? Winnie tries on men and casts them aside like clothes from a department store bargain rack. I'll bet Winnie sleeps nights. At least I have my Alices project to fill my days. Oh, I mustn't forget to pick up the new cards in the morning. Forget? How could I forget?*

WINNIE

Winnie Flemming was first to see the new proxy cards. Jessica had dropped one on her desk and asked, "Isn't it beautiful?" It had been nearly three weeks since Winnie's birthday party.

"You and Donna did a super job, Jess." Winnie turned over the new card in her hand. "It looks enough like the old one to pass at a distance. I guess you know the Bleeper is near-sighted, don't you?" she added. "Yet, everything is here. The new committee, the new signature space, date line, everything. Wow, it's like holding a beautiful stick of dynamite when you think about it." Winnie looked up at Jessica. "It scares me a little."

"It scares me a lot. Yet, we're not doing anything illegal, immoral, or fattening," Jessica added, "Let's go get a cup of coffee."

"Now that's illegal!" Winnie tucked the card into a folder and carefully placed the folder in her desk drawer. Conversation was limited, almost stilted, as the two women headed for the coffee shop. "Gee I wish we could take coffee to our desks. It seems so silly to enforce all these stupid rules. I never could understand why the Bleeper says no coffee drinking at our desks. It doesn't make any more sense than the nine-thirty rule. He breaks it himself when he feels like an early cup." Winnie held the door for her friend.

"Actually not," Jessica whispered. "He drinks tea. That's power, Winnie. Rules, wily rules, whether or not they make sense, just to keep the workers in place."

The women poured their coffee and moved to a corner of the room, selecting a table near the wall. Jessica sat down and casually inquired, "How was your birthday? I don't think we've had a chance to talk since."

"It turned into a whiz-bang weekend. I've met this terrific guy... or did I tell you about Randy? He has an apartment that is decorated in modern-modern — you know, in black and white, rather stark, but cushy, the most comfortable place I've ever seen. Mounds of pillows and soft furniture, and this dog. He has a dog that gets jealous every time I come over."

"How long has this been going on?"

"Well, I met him the night of my birthday party. After work, a bunch of us went to the Green Room for a couple of drinks, and he was tending bar. Everyone else left and I sat and talked to him until closing, and then we went to his place. I guess you knew Don and I broke up."

"I'm not sure I knew Don. Really, Winnie, you change men so often it's hard to keep track. I don't see how you do it, with your daughter living with you and all."

"Becka isn't aware of my social life. Besides, I never bring them home. She's usually asleep when I get in anyway. No, she's okay."

"Okay," Jessica repeated, then realized she wanted to say something close to judgmental. She moved away from the subject. "So, you celebrated your birthday weekend with… what's his name?"

"Randy. Becka had gone to an all-night slumber party so we had the whole weekend. I feel so giddy when I think about it. We just did silly things, but he is so much fun. He has this monstrous hot tub, and we drank wine and…"

"Winnie, are you sure you want to tell me all of this?"

"I don't mind. In fact, I just have to share it with somebody. It's so wonderful being with someone to have a good time, but it's even more fun having someone to tell it to, you know?"

"Not really. Are you two serious? Do you think this will be a lasting relationship?"

"O god no! I'm not ready for a lasting relationship. My counselor says I shouldn't even think about it until the divorce is at least two years old. And it's only been, what, seven months?"

"I think what your shrink was suggesting was for you to sit back and assess your life and yourself during that time, and take it easy with these intimate affairs… or relationships." Jessica knew she was on judgmental ground now, but she liked Winnie and wasn't comfortable hearing about these hedonistic headlong dives into meaningless affairs.

"My shrink doesn't know about Randy. Or Don either, for that matter. It's none of her business."

"But what the hell are you going to her for if you won't let her in on your problems?"

"I can't call Randy a problem. I just don't think it's any of her business."

"But it *is* her business, Winnie. That is her business, to help you with your relationships and to help you deal with yourself. Better you tell *her* about your weekend in a hot tub rather than me."

"Easy for you to say," Winnie's voice rose. "You don't get tied into relationships with people like I do."

"I'm not sure how you mean that, but I'll take it at face value. Simmer down, Winnie. Cool off. Let yourself get strong again after the divorce before you go running around looking for love in every bar in town." Jessica reached over and gently touched Winnie's arm.

"But I need someone, Jess. I'm not the kind of woman who likes to sleep alone. I need someone with me. I was married for fourteen years! I got used to it before that bastard took off with little miss what's-her-name. I feel lost, and alone, and I don't like it. If I had my way I would get married again… just as fast as I can find someone. So I'm looking. What's wrong with that?"

"Nothing, Winnie, nothing is wrong. Just don't be in such a hurry. There's a real nice guy out there somewhere, and he'll find you, if you don't find him first. But you won't know him if you keep jumping into bed with every guy that comes along. In time, you won't know the difference between the good ones and the bad."

"And until that happens, I'm supposed to sit home and get old. No thanks; I'll keep up the search. It gives me something to do."

The subject seemed to be closed. Winnie had her needs; let her live her life her way. Jessica was anxious to get off the psychoanalysis trail. She wouldn't ever be able to convince Winnie she was searching wildly for something that must happen by itself in its own good time. Meanwhile, Winnie was skilled at her job and serious about it, and a heated problem at work would keep her busy.

"Speaking of things to do," Jessica finally said, "we have to plan a trip to the branches, Winnie, to let them see the new proxies. Can we take a bunch over to Terri's office tomorrow morning?"

"Sure, let's combine it with a quicky inventory of customer giveaways. That will give us a valid reason to be there, if anybody notices."

"Good." Jessica took her cup to the sink. Winnie followed. As they replaced cups on the shelf, Jessica winked at her friend and said loudly, "Nine o'clock tomorrow, Winnie — we'll go to Central Branch first for inventory check. I'll take care of getting the company car. See you."

"Winnie smiled. There wasn't anybody around to be interested in where they went or what they did. Everybody at Stateside Bank seemed to have problems of their own.

The next morning it was way after nine before they left. The Bleeper had called Jessica in for some minor matter about eight-thirty. He liked to perform before an audience. While Jessica sat and twiddled her thumbs, he did his big-man-on-telephone routine for her benefit, pushing his speaker button so she could hear both sides of the conversation. Branch people always knew who was calling when they heard his crackly voice. It sounded like someone calling from inside a very small box. He didn't fool anyone, although he often tried. That morning he called Terri, and Jessica smiled at the branch manager's pretended reaction, "Who is calling, please?" Jessica thought, she knows damned well who is calling. After he completed that call, he placed three more, turning off the speaker only when he wasn't showing off.

Between her own phone calls and other interruptions, Jessica was late picking up the car and Winnie. When they reached Terri's office, they all had a good laugh about the telephone scam. "He thinks we don't recognize that little-box voice," Terri smiled. "But nobody else sounds like that. At least we have a warning system when he's on the line."

"Want to see something pretty?" Jessica changed the subject. She reached into her brief case and pulled out the folder with the new proxy cards. Handing one to Terri, she asked, "Want to be the first to sign?"

"Why not?" Terri reached for a pen. "Hey, I have an idea. Why not sign the card, but leave the date open. Then, if there is any question, we can date them later if we have to."

"I don't think so," Jessica replied. "Better date it today, then if necessary, you can sign another later. But I can't see why that should be necessary. Donna said that the latest date on the proxy counts. Just don't sign a company proxy after today."

The women laughed easily as Terri ceremoniously signed the proxy and handed it back to Jessica. "The first ticket for Alice," she said.

"And here's the second," added Winnie.

"And the third," said Jessica, pulling a card toward her and signing it.

Project Alices was underway.

TERRI

Terri Litton-Clark was sure the plan would work. Frankly, if it didn't and she was out of a job, there was no big deal. She was flexible; why sweat it.

After Winnie and Jessica left, the attractive young woman sat back for a moment and thought about her career track until now. She had worked for a figure-improving parlor for six months, then had moved into selling memberships in an athletic club. It helped to have a good body, especially since she was nearing that magical thirtieth year.

But there wasn't much money to be made in the body business. She remembered the management courses she had taken before she lucked into the job at Stateside Savings. Not an illustrious career so far, but a promising one if you took into consideration the guts it took to tell Stateside's personnel department that she had held management positions as a supervisor. She also was able to imply she had a degree in business. They believed her. She figured correctly that, based on the low pay they offered her, they probably wouldn't bother checking.

She had no doubts she could handle the job, so she had no real problem with the lies, just the chance that someday somebody might ask questions about her past that she couldn't answer truthfully.

Terri was a scrapper, no denying that, which prepared her well for the scrap that she knew would ensue when she called together her staff at Central Branch to tell them about the Alices. She would have to tread lightly, as if she were walking on a swaying suspension bridge. She knew her people and she knew how to handle them.

Furthermore, she looked the part that day. Anyone at Stateside would identify her dark navy uniform as power dressing. The darker the navy, the higher the office — everyone knew that, even though it wasn't written down anywhere. She had even chosen a tie instead of a scarf for an authoritative accent.

Terri called the staff meeting at the close of the day. Although the tellers were anxious to get home, they were in a playful mood as they gathered in the lobby. Most grabbed soft drinks from the machines; some poured cups of coffee. This was a large branch, and about eighteen women were seated in front of her when Terri began.

She moved slowly, carefully, around the room, looking each employee straight in the eye, trying to show she was fully in command and expecting every woman in the room to follow loyally. Good thing there weren't any men at Central — but that was Bleeper's choice, to keep the men in the mortgage department and in administration. Men wouldn't accept this technique of directness from a woman.

"A matter has come up that requires all of us to cooperate fully in a project that can benefit each and every one of us. It requires your full cooperation, which is what I am asking for. If you prefer not to work with this project, I am asking for your silence. Your silence will show your respect for me and what we have developed in this branch."

Terri knew her people well. She knew that each of the tellers was super-proud of the branch record they had established. They had a right to be. When Terri took over, this was the largest branch in size and the lowest in actual dollar figures. Terri had created a team who brought the numbers back up and who were proud of their achievements; together the team had held onto the top spot with a ferocity never before demonstrated at Stateside. Terri was the proudest of all.

That evening she laid out the plan, giving her team as much information as she felt they needed to make a decision. The women were smiling as she concluded.

"Well, will you help put a woman in the Board Room?" she asked at last.

The tellers looked at each other uneasily and nodded, but no one spoke. Until the head teller began, "Sure, Terri, you can count on me." The litany continued, "You can count on me, Terri." "I'll help." "Right with you, Terri."

At first.

Then someone, a new staff member, asked innocently, "What happens if it doesn't work? Could we lose our jobs?"

Terri was taking a breath to answer when another voice said, "Maybe we could be black-balled in the banking business and never get another job. You know, sort of marked for life as a troublemaker or worse, a rebel or traitor."

"I don't think that would be likely." Terri tried to calm the voices that were beginning to grow louder. "Sure, you need to know you possibly could lose your jobs, but that isn't the issue. The issue is whether or not you will work with us on this. We will do everything possible to take the heat if something goes wrong." Terri had raised her voice. "We'll also do everything possible to see that nothing does go wrong."

Then, "I don't even think this is legal. I don't think we ought to get involved."

Terri had identified the persistent voice of doubt. She looked directly at her, "Don't worry, Debbie. From the way your work has been going lately, I'm not really sure you will even be here at annual meeting time." Whether this was taken as a threat or a mere statement of fact, it seemed to work. After that, Debbie sat quietly, shaking her head from time to time and glowering at Terri. The opposition had melted, and Terri finally continued answering questions about the project operation details.

Debbie would take watching. The other tellers listened to Terri's presentation and accepted a handful of proxy cards. They had agreed to keep the cards in a special place in their work drawers, out of immediate sight, but available for customers. They chatted among themselves for a moment, planning ways to handle the security of these precious documents. Most of the tellers finally decided to place the cards beneath a few of the old proxies, marking them with a divider of another color or with a paper clip. They talked quietly, but excitedly, like conspirators planning a dangerous plot. They were, after all, weren't they?

"Recognize the power that you tellers have as a consolidated group," Terri reminded them as they concluded the meeting. "Realize that if we all work as one, there is a good chance of achieving our goal to offset the power that is working from the top. We have the power of numbers if we use it."

As the tellers walked toward their stations to tuck away the proxy cards, Terri could see the power that she had talked about. The power of women taking control of their lives. In the end they can be the final controlling power. They are beautiful.

KEEPING YOUR EYES OPEN

Some tagged it the "daily sacrifice of a Christian".

Every morning the senior officers of Stateside Savings Bank met to discuss the day's work. And every morning the Bleeper threw a tantrum. Like a daily cathartic, the tantrum was a ritualistic cleansing that was forgotten as soon as it had worked its wonders.

Like the sacrifice of a Christian to a pagan god, the ritual had become fairly commonplace, and the staff grew to expect it. "Has he had his morning Christian?" an approaching vice president would ask Talcott's secretary Ann. Nobody wanted to be the first in the den.

Of course, Tom Talcott hadn't heard the phrase. He would have sacrificed another "Christian" if he had.

The regularity and the certainty of the ritual did not diminish its violence. And no one was exempt for long. The target of the ritual didn't matter. All Talcott felt was the need to release the pressure inside him every morning.

Upon arising each day, his head would begin to fill with things that needed doing at the office. He'd listen to the bank's radio commercial on the seven o'clock news while he shaved, and the ideas would begin to flood his head — ideas for better marketing, better investments, better ways to bring in more money. "Why don't my people come up with these ideas?" he'd ask his mirrored reflection. "Why must I do everything myself?"

The two-mile walk to the office was not only physically invigorating, but it stimulated even more creative thought. By the time Talcott entered the office he was bubbling with ideas — ideas that he thought he alone felt, that only he was conscientious enough or caring enough to come up with.

And why not? It was his bank. He had built it from that lackadaisical welfare office his father had left him. Now he controlled a multi-million-dollar thriving business that had been making big profits since the third year after the Senior Talcott died. Talcott took home an annual bonus amounting to more than his highest officer's annual salary. Talcott hired; Talcott fired; Talcott ruled by himself. The pressure increased.

That day he had decided to offer a gigantic giveaway program to open the third quarter, one like the bank hadn't done since before deregulation. He was going to give away a trip around the world and advertise it as the result one could expect from banking with a friendly place like Stateside. *Why hadn't Operations or Marketing seen this obvious promotional idea?*

The plan was pulsating throughout his head when Marketing Director Jessica Nadeau tapped on his door. "Hi, Chief," she smiled, "Have a minute?"

"Sure, come on in," he smiled back. "Just the person I want to see. How's your mom?"

"Just fine," replied Jessica, thinking, *Mom has been out of the hospital for eight months. When will he stop asking?* "What I need is authorization to run a market study on the thirty-day investment certificates — like we talked about last week. We…"

"Investment certificates!" Talcott bellowed. He sounded astounded, "We don't want to sell investment certificates in this market. Why would we want to run a market study on them?"

"But I thought you…"

"Recognition! Identification! That's what we need in this overly competitive market. Let's concentrate on making the name of Stateside Savings a household word. Let's run a market study on that!" His voice rose as he mimicked Jessica's words.

"I was only…" she began to defend herself. He had asked for the market study only three days earlier. Now that she was prepared to give it to him, he had changed his mind. The irrational pattern was familiar!

The tirade that followed also was an old familiar story: "I can't believe you're earning a living in marketing, much less as a marketing director. How can you be so damned stupid? Don't you get paid for coming up with ideas we can use to get more customers in here?"

Jessica braced herself. She realized with a start that she was the day's sacrificial Christian. *I won't cry*, she thought. *Here it comes. He'd love it if he thought he could get to me, make me cry, but not this time!*

"I want you to get yourself back to your desk and complete a marketing program to outline a gigantic giveaway, a trip around the world for a lucky customer — a contest, a drawing, you figure out the details. I want it today," he thundered. "I want radio, television, newspaper — all the media — no, let's use direct mail and hit all our loyal customers. Never mind looking for new business with this. I want..."

No sense even trying to talk him out of this, Jessica thought. I'll not even mention budget. He knows it's not in there this quarter. The same old routine. She knew it so well: go back to her office, work up his program, hand him the cost sheet and watch him change his mind. It had happened that way before... many times before.

"Now get out of here," the president had finished his tirade. "It's nearly time for the Senior Officers' meeting. I haven't looked at the agenda yet."

"Okay, Chief." Jessica smiled, or tried to. Another day shot, she thought. Maybe by meeting time he'll have changed his mind. No, don't even hope. It's another lost day. But what the hell, it's his money and he's spending it. Tack up another battle star!

As she fled the battlefield, she passed the incoming officer team. "He's all yours," the battered Christian muttered.

Jessica headed for the elevator, her thoughts rushing wildly together with the current of her emotions. Then she noticed Debbie, the teller from Terri's branch office.

"Hi, Debbie, what brings you into Corporate this morning?" she asked casually. Behind the facade of surprise, Jessica hid her suspicions for Debbie's visit. Terri had reported the feisty teller's reaction to the staff meeting, and Jessica had kept her eyes open.

"Nothing special, I hope. Mr. Talcott sent for me," she lied. "I guess it couldn't be all that bad... at least I hope not." She was babbling. Jessica knew, of course, that Talcott never sends for tellers, and never at Senior Officers' meeting time.

Jessica watched the powder blue uniform move gingerly toward the secretary's desk. She watched as Debbie pleaded with Ann for an audience with Mr. Talcott. After several minutes, the teller turned back toward the elevator, unaware that Jessica watched from the corner.

The elevator doors closed behind Debbie before Jessica crossed the room to Ann's desk. "She said she had some 'important information about the branch meeting'," Ann mimicked the young teller. "I told her I would forward any information she had, but she chose not to share with me," the secretary smiled.

"Good work, Ann," Jessica replied. "I sure feel glad you're on our side."

"Side nothing," she smiled sweetly. "I'm just doing my job — keeping Mr. Talcott safe from trouble-making employees." She grinned at Jessica and stuck her thumb upward in the air.

"A new marketing program," Jessica muttered to herself as she climbed wearily into her car that evening. It was nearly six o'clock and she was mentally and emotionally drained. She checked her rolled-up windows and screamed all the way home, cursing her job, her boss, her bank, her life. She screamed so loudly and so long that her voice was scratchy when she entered the house. A small expense for a more controlled disposition, she thought.

"Hi, gang," she managed in an almost cheerful tone. Sorry I'm late." She nearly walked past Dan who sat quietly at the kitchen table. "Dan, oh, Dan, you don't know how happy I am to see you." She was near tears as she threw her arms around his neck.

"Well, I'll have to remember to turn up late more often."

"Late? Are you late?" Jessica looked at the clock. "Didn't you say your plane would be here... right... at... five." She remembered then. "How'd you get here? Who met your plane? Oh Dan, I'm so sorry. It's been a dreadful day and..."

Dan cut her short with another kiss and held her close as he reassured her, "It's okay; I rented a car. The kids and I have had a lovely talk, and we've nibbled the supper nearly to death, and now you're home. Safe. That's all that matters."

"You weren't worried, were you?" Jess pulled back and looked at his face. She could see that he was. "The kids know that I can get held up for a dozen reasons, and they don't worry about me. I guess you'll have to learn. As long as I have this job, you can't depend on me for anything."

"Then we may have to consider getting you out of that job."

"Not while I'm earning this salary. It's too good to throw away."

"But if it's costing you your sanity…"

"Sanity? Sanity?" Jessica rolled over the words slowly. Sanity. Is that what is being threatened? The thought that followed brought a smile to her face. The sanest thing I've ever done is to begin the Alices Project. That's where the sanity begins.

The remainder of the evening was filled with family. Jess and Dan became the perfect parents, helping with homework and listening to the events of Amy's school day. Just as Amy went off to bed, Richard asked if they would listen to a report on Watergate he had to give in school the next day.

"I can remember exactly where I listened to Nixon's farewell speech," Dan told Jessica after Richard had left them alone. "I was sitting in the waiting room of St. Joseph Hospital in Portland trying to keep my mind busy while my son was being born."

"You miss your children, don't you," Jessica said.

"Yes. Very much. Did I tell you, my attorney says Nora will consider giving me custody if I move back here, back west?"

"Are you considering that? Do you want custody?"

"Why yes. I thought you knew that."

"But Dan, they're growing up. Another few years they'll be off on their own. Do you want to upset your job, your life, for those few years?"

"I'm not sure you can understand, since you have your children with you. I miss those kids. I miss their quarreling, their victories, their noise, their tears, their laughter. I just plain miss them. Teddy is only twelve and Danielle is just entering high school. Bradley won't graduate for two more years. Those few years you mention are some very precious years for me. Jess, can we spend some time this summer together, all together. Can we find a beach house and bring my three up to spend a couple weeks with you, me, Amy, and

Richard? I know it will be hard. I think I know what we're in for. But we could have some good times."

"Dan, are you crazy? All those bubbling teenage hormones under one roof... with us? Are you out of your mind?" The subject of sanity was rearing its head for the second time this evening. "No. That definitely is not a good idea. Definitely. Not. Good."

"Jess, it would mean so much just to give it a try."

"No, Dan. First of all, my son and yours are not alike. Besides the two years in age, Brad is a... a jock. Richard is not. Plus you have two daughters that fall in Richard's hormonal range. And what if your sixteen-year-old Bradley took a shine to my Amy? Worse, what if they all fought each other?"

"Jess, no. You're grasping at problems that aren't there. Or may not be there. I realize there might be problems, but that would be part of our expectations, and I'm sure we could handle them. We might even have fun handling them. Ma and Pa handling their house full of kids."

"Sorry, Dan. I want a vacation that is restful, not challenging. I *need* a vacation that is restful. No. My answer is no."

Dan gave up trying. "So, tell me about your day," he continued, reaching over to switch off the lamp. "Tell me what the big bad boogyman did to make you scream all the way home."

"You knew?"

"Of course. You told me once how you scream to let off steam. And when you walked in tonight, your voice was absolutely hoarse. Long scream home?"

"Yes. The boss has me doing an entire new campaign. But we all know it isn't budgeted, so it will be a futile one. I just wish he'd..."

"Why not use the time to design a campaign like you'd really want to see happen. Design one that would be state-of-the-art if the old boy appreciated art. Then you'll have it to send off in your portfolio when you look for another job."

"Not a bad idea. Hmmm. Not bad at all. Thanks. I'll do it. I just may be looking for another job before long."

"That sounds hopeful. Can I hope?"

"What do you mean *hope*? I may lose my job."

"Oh Jess, you say that all the time. You can handle the old man."

"You don't know the half of it. I'm not kidding about my job." She proceeded to tell him the whole story of the Alices Project, all their plans and their progress.

Dan listened patiently, then smiled broadly and said, "Well, it's about time! At last, somebody is taking on the old boy. I'd give anything to have this work and see the look on his face. I tell you, Jess, whoever came up with this idea should get a medal." Then seeing the look on her face, he added, "Naw, you? Really? Well, I'm impressed. I should have guessed."

Dan stayed through the weekend. The question of summer vacations together didn't come up again until late Sunday, just before he hopped on the plane heading back to Chicago. "Jess, will you at least think over my suggestion for summer vacation? Just think about it one more time, please?"

"No need to think, Dan. It just wouldn't work. Besides, I'm not sure I'll even get a summer vacation. I may not be able to get away until after the fall quarterlies. If he suspects I'm taking a few days off, the boss will find things for me to do. I keep my plans quiet until I can get clean away."

"That's no way to live, Jess. You have to get out of there. Why not start looking now?"

"I don't know, Dan. The money is good. I don't want to jeopardize that until I have a chance to look around." Jessica was holding Dan's arm tightly. "Let's leave my office out of this. Let's just talk about you and me. Next time we get together, no office, just us. Okay?"

"Sure. But I'm not sure they're not tied together. Very tightly."

"They're calling you to board, sweetheart. Have a good flight. Call me when you get home."

"It'll be late."

"That's okay. I just like to hear your voice before I go to sleep. Bye."

"See you soon. I love you, Jess."

The summer passed as Jessica feared it would. Each time she penned in her vacation time, Talcott found a project that *just had to be done.* She gave up trying for a block of time and settled for a couple very long weekends. Five days here, five days there. She and Dan spent them together as often as he could get out of Chicago. Once he had to cancel because he couldn't get on an overbooked flight. Later flights wouldn't have given them much time together. It was not the summer he had planned.

It wasn't the summer Jess had planned either. Will called her twice, once to tell her the divorce was going along smoothly, the other to tell her that his family was begging him to call it off. Autumn didn't look that much better. The Alices project was taking up more and more of her time, both on the job and off.

After her brush with Debbie, Jessica's work took on new meaning. She spent more time moving from one branch to another, making friends throughout the system. Friends and trustworthy people were key elements, and Jessica meant to develop them. Everywhere she went, tellers held up their fingers showing the recent tally of new proxies. As the weeks passed, each time she returned to a branch, they were eager to show her larger and larger numbers. After Labor Day, the Fall Operations Meetings seeped into her busy schedule. Jessica had to plan the regular quarterly regional meetings to update branch personnel with exactly what was going on at Corporate, what was being (officially) planned. This time, she grinned to herself. There would be two levels of planning, with only one visible to the troops.

The gigantic world trip giveaway was quashed as soon as Talcott saw how much the promotion would cost. The market survey that followed (Jessica had anticipated him for once and was ready) showed that additional deposits might come in with emphasis on the Direct Deposits program.

The Direct Deposits program was Judy's department, giving her the opportunity to work closely with Jessica to plan the upcoming regional meetings. Judy was an expert in reaching personnel departments and making attractive offers they couldn't refuse. Now all she had to do was pass on to the branch people all she knew, to help them accomplish the same thing.

Time was short and the meetings were approaching fast. Jessica took a cue from the Bleeper and called a meeting for the first thing

Monday, nine a.m. She figured they could get the whole thing planned at one sitting and not waste a lot of company time.

"Be on time, Judy," Jessica had chided as the staff headed for the parking lot Friday night. Judy had an absent-minded way of showing up late for meetings, sometimes even for work.

"No problem," Judy called back. "Nothing special going on this weekend. Just some quiet time with the family. I'll be bright and early… well, at least early."

JUDY

On Monday, most of the places around the conference table were filled by one minute before nine when Judy Robertson skittered through the door. She was rushing as usual, yellow pad tucked under her arm.

"Hey, what happened to you?" Jessica asked. "That's a beaut!" She referred to a large bruise on Judy's right cheek. It was carefully covered with makeup, but there was no hiding it. As she looked closer, Jessica saw Judy's swollen eye and a cut near her eyebrow that was beginning to crust over.

"Some damn fool driver shot out of a side street on my way home Friday. I slammed on the brakes, about went through the windshield, but he missed me." Judy offered the explanation almost casually and her co-workers seemed to buy it.

"Let's get down to business," Jessica began.

Papers were handed around the table. Winnie leaned over and whispered to Jessica, "That S.O.B. let her have it again this weekend. How much longer is she going to take that stuff?"

The meeting underway, Judy settled back, aware that Jessica had seen and understood. At least there would be someone she could talk to, someone who would understand the way it was with Hank. But should she talk about this one? This time it was different. This time he didn't care if he hit her where the bruises would show. This time he wasn't thinking about her going back to work and facing her colleagues.

"Don't go to work today," Hank had begged this morning. "Phone in sick. That won't show in another day." Always afterward he was apologetic, almost sweet.

"But I have to be there today; we have a nine o'clock meeting and they're depending on me," she had told him. "It doesn't hurt much and I can put makeup on it. Besides, nobody notices my bruises anymore. They all think I'm accident-prone."

"You haven't told anyone, have you?" Hank looked worried.

"No," Judy lied. "It's no one's business. I've wanted to, Hank. I can't handle this alone. I can't keep up the lies at the office. What's worse I can't keep lying to myself. What's wrong with me that makes you turn on me like you do?"

Hank had hold of her shoulder and was trying to offer comfort, but she didn't feel his arm. She was numb, remembering only the pain of the battering she had taken just hours before.

"I'm sorry, babe. I told you that. You know how I am. I don't know what happens. Maybe I drink too much. Yeah, maybe I ought to join AA or something. Maybe…"

"That's not a bad idea, Hank," Judy raised her head and faced him. "I'm serious. I think you do need help. If you only…"

"No!" Hank shouted, pulling back his hands. "No, I don't need help. We can handle our own problems. Not that this is a problem, but we can handle it."

"Okay, simmer down. It's late. I better get going."

"Don't go to work, babe. Stay home today."

"No, I have to go, Hank." Judy started for the door.

"Okay, you go, but don't you blow off about us, you hear! If I find out you've told anyone, I'll really let you have it. Understand?"

"I understand, Hank. 'I walked into a door!' No, I've used that one." Judy would have smiled, but her face hurt. "There's plenty of potato salad left in the fridge. And see that the kids take their vitamins."

"Yeah, sure." Hank turned from the door and headed back to the bedroom. Judy closed the door, glanced at her watch, and hurried to the car.

The meeting ran longer than planned and it was past coffee break time when it ended. Judy needed a cup of coffee and headed for the lunchroom. Nobody from Operations was there, thank god. She could enjoy her coffee without conversation.

But the thoughts remained, that hideous scene floating to the foreground, receding, returning sharply into focus. Judy's hand let go of the warm cup and moved lightly across the bruised cheek.

The sting of his hand suddenly was fresh on her face. She felt it again as strongly as the first time. He had lashed out at her, first with words, then with his rocklike hand.

"Your place is here feeding these kids, washing their goddamn clothes, taking care of them… and me," he had yelled at her. "What is so damned great about that fuckin' office that takes up so much of your time?" Without waiting for answers, he began the litany of accusations, all the reasons that fueled his anger, all the reasons that gave him cause to hit her.

"Must be somebody down there more important than your husband and kids." His voice grew shrill, accusing. "Must be something down there that means more'n your family. Well, we won't stand for it. I care too much for these kids to let their mom go whore'n around some goddamn office six nights a week. Maybe if I let you know how much we feel, you can find more time to do your work here, where you belong.

"I don't want no more night work down there, you hear? No more leaving us alone!" And as the last words spewed from his angry mouth, his hand caught the side of her face, pushing her head sideways, leaving his hand imprint on her cheek. "No more leaving us *alone!*" He hit her again as he repeated "alone". God, how he hated to be alone with those kids!

"Can I join you? or do you want to be alone?" a voice cut into the scene in Judy's head.

"Alone?" she answered aloud. "No, I don't want to be alone."

Then she saw Jessica as she placed her cup on the table next to Judy's and sat down. Softly she asked, "Wanna talk?"

Thanks, Jess, but it's the same story you've heard before. Only this time it hurt more. Physically, I mean. I guess I've got used to the inside bruises."

"Why don't you leave him? He's not doing you any good. And what happens when he starts batting the kids around? You can take it, sure. Well, some of it, but how about them?"

This was a question Judy hadn't considered. "He wouldn't touch them. He loves them."

"You told me once he'd never hit you — back when he started all this ranting and raving about your job, when he was first out of work, remember? Now look at you."

"Does it show that much? Do you think anybody else knows?" Judy looked worried. And the expression she saw on Jessica's face told her she wasn't kidding anyone. "They all know, don't they?"

"Leave him, Judy," Jessica repeated. "Before he gets more violent."

"Where would I go? I don't have enough money to stretch now. Where could I go that I could afford?" There was a pause while Judy thought. She stood up abruptly. "Besides, Hank couldn't get along by himself. He needs me."

The subject was closed.

The subject of abuse was closed, settled for Judy. But it lingered at the back of Jessica's mind.

Who is battering who? she asked herself that night alone in her bedroom. I'm willing to admit that Will is a kind of batterer. He keeps me dangling. He knows I'm in love with him, that I'll do just about anything he asks and keep coming back for more. Why else would I have waited so long, bought his excuses, listened to his promises? He knows I'm always here, always available when he decides... when *he* decides. He decides, not me. He calls when *he* decides to talk to me. He comes to see me when *he* decides. He decides. The words were turning obscene, angry in her head. *He decides.*

Jessica! She woke herself up. Jessica, you are Will's toy. He is playing with you the same as he plays with... every... other... woman he knows. Like an explosion, the realization broke into a giant mushroom cloud that she no longer could avoid. "You mean nothing to him," she said aloud. There, alone in her darkened room, Jessica understood the battering she had been giving herself at Will's whim. "And I let him do it." That was the difficult part to accept. "I let him do it." The tears began to roll softly into her pillow, and continued until they were gone.

What to do about it now is the quandary. Jessica argued with herself. What do I do now? I could call him in the middle of the night, disturb him, wake him up with a call from me. That would be a switch. Or I can wait until he calls me.

No, no more waiting. It's time you took your life into your own hands. How could you do this to Dan, withhold a part of yourself to wait for this bum who has dangled you for… how many years? We won't count. How could you give Dan hope for your future together and hold Will out as a trump card you might need later?

There's no choice. This is not a matter of choice. Dan is the man I love. I have to tell Will before… before he divorces his wife for me?

Ha! I don't believe that will ever happen. But if it should? Wouldn't you just love to think you had the power to break up that marriage? Ha! again. I think you're awake now, Jess. Let's test it. Phone Will now, tonight. Tell him you're through, you're out of his life… forever.

Let's not. Let's just leave things the way they are until he calls again. Then I can tell him. Besides, his wife might pick up the phone.

The argument ended. It wasn't a satisfactory decision for Jess, but at least it marked a realization that all was not rosy in Hope Heaven. She would have to choose, sooner or later, and the choice meant telling Will goodbye. She wasn't ready yet.

Yes, I will tell Will goodbye and commit to being with Dan. The next time he calls, I'll tell Dan I've decided… marriage. Gee, that feels good.

POWER DECISIONS

Power decisions are made in a number of ways. Sometimes a decision requires mounds of research, study, and contemplation. Sometimes a decision is based on intuition and comes at the snap of a finger. On occasion, a decision is made when no other possibility offers itself. Then there is the decision that seems to be made somewhere else and presents itself at the last moment.

Jessica's decision to marry Dan was a composite of all these methods. Surely, she had enough research to know that Will was an unsure, unreliable, un-everything man who would eventually break her heart. His track record was obvious to Jessica now.

If Jess felt intuitive, it was her excitement at hearing Dan's voice a few nights later that made her sure she was making the right choice. Besides, if the truth were known, there just wasn't any other decision.

However, Jessica's choice was altered by the kind of decision that seems to be made elsewhere and presented at the right moment.

"Hi, Jess. I'm calling to tell you a decision that I've come to."

"I know, Dan. I know. And I'm willing to…"

"Don't interrupt until I'm finished, please Jess. This is difficult enough for me."

"You sound so serious," Jessica chided. She felt a happy, teasing mood overcome her with the relief in her decision to marry Dan.

"I am serious, Jess. More serious than I've ever been. And I should have done this long ago."

"Now you've got me curious. Done what?"

"Told you… said that…" Dan's words weren't coming out the way he wanted them to. "Jessica, I'm through. I mean, we can't go on. I mean, Jessica, I won't be calling you any more or coming to see you. I can't. Not any more."

Silence. Dead silence. The grin on Jessica's face froze. Dan's fumbling words stopped. Only the hum of the telephone wire and some shadow of sound remained in their ears.

"Dan, you don't mean this. You can't. I've decided that you and I…"

"No, Jess. Whatever you've decided is too late. I have to get on with my life and I can't wait forever for you to make up your mind to accept my love and me into your life. Your work is too important for you to take the time for me. I realize that now. It always will be that way. Your priorities are different than mine. I guess that's what I fell in love with. But now, it's an impediment. You just don't love me enough to see who I am or what I need from you. Or maybe you just don't want to. Anyway, I've made this decision and I won't be calling you again. Goodbye, Jess."

"Dan, please don't go. Don't hang up until I've told you…"

"Sorry, sweetheart. I can't talk any more. I'll always love you. Goodbye." Click.

This is a nightmare, Jess thought. I'll wake up soon. Please, god, let me wake up. He can't mean it. He'll call back in a few minutes. He'll know how much this hurts me. He'll care. He'll want to be sure I'm all right. Please, god, let him call back and say he didn't mean it. How can this be?

The tears came with the realization that the phone wasn't going to ring again. It's over. He means it. Oh Dan, Dan. You'll never know how much I love you. You'll never know how much you mean to me. When the sobs finally subsided and sleep came, Jessica had a chilled empty space inside her that she carried around for days.

Jessica didn't realize that she hadn't thought of Will for those three days after Dan's call. She wouldn't have thought of him then if it hadn't been for the note on her desk. "Will call tonight — good news. Will."

Then she remembered she was going to call him and tell him goodbye. Maybe if she had, Dan's call would have been hers. My god, Dan said to me the things that I should have been saying to

Will. I guess this is my punishment for... The thought was left incomplete.

Is the picture any different now? I wish I could talk this over with someone. But who? Dan was my closest friend. Who else would understand? Judy would tell me, in fact she already told me, that Will is a bum, a romantic deadbeat. Winnie would tell me to go out looking for someone entirely new. Donna would have me crawling back to one of them. Sheila? Maybe Sheila.

"No, this is something you have to work out for yourself, Jess. You're the only one who can direct your life. This is your life, kiddo," she told herself. And for the first time in days, she smiled.

When Will called, it usually was about midnight. Jess imagined him sitting in a dressing gown in his study. She imagined he read or listened to music through a pleasant evening, then turned to the phone for the comfort of her voice. (More probably, he waited for his wife to go to bed before reaching for the phone.)

Tonight would be different. Jessica was armed with the finality of her decision. Tonight *she* would make the decisions. She would make the call. About ten-thirty (after her children were asleep), she dialed Will's number.

"Hello." His voice sounded sleepy. Or had he been drinking? "Hello," he repeated.

"Hi. It's me, J..." then she paused. Would he recognize her voice? He should after hearing it these many years. Let's just find out. "It's me," she pitched her voice a bit higher and left it at that.

"Oh hi. How are you? What are you doing?" Will chose his words carefully. Jess was sure he didn't know who he was talking to. If he had that many women friends, he might be fishing for clues. He was. "Tell me, how was your day?" he asked.

"Oh so-so. I just couldn't wait to hear your voice," she teased. "How are you coming with the plan you mentioned last time we talked?" she asked. She was enjoying this.

"I don't remember where we left off. Refresh my memory," he dodged.

"You know, the divorce, the wedding," she replied.

"Oh, darling, it's just as we left it. I can't get my wife to leave the children, and I know how much you want them with us."

"Why Will, we never discussed having the children with us? Who the hell do you think you're talking to?"

"Why... who... isn't this...? I mean, who is this?"

Jessica was furious. She would have liked to make him wonder and sweat much longer, but she couldn't contain the anger that was rumbling through her insides. "You wimp, you worm, you miserable low-life. Do you have so many women you can't keep them straight?"

She didn't wait for his reply. Indeed, he was speechless anyway. "There was a time I thought you really cared for me. I thought ours was the love of a lifetime. Maybe it was. But it has died. Any love that I may have felt for you in the past is dead, dead, dead. And that's the way I wish you were, dead, dead, dead. As far as I'm concerned you are... dead. I shall not call you ever again. And you are not to call me — ever. If you try to contact me, I shall go immediately to your wife and then to my lawyer to bring charges against you. Goodbye."

Jessica slammed the phone down, put her head down and cried, thick cleansing tears. Her entire body seemed to be ridding itself of the wasted tears of a finished love. When the crying stopped, she slept soundly, deeply, her body feeling the freedom that came from a good decision well executed.

The next morning driving to work, she felt re-born, new. The sadness of Dan's decision was offset by the exhilaration of her decision about Will. Now she could continue to exert her own control over her own life. Now she knew she was making decisions for herself. This was a heady power and she was loving it.

Not until she was pulling into her parking space did she realize she had never identified herself to Will during their phone conversation. She went over the dialog carefully. No, not once did he know for sure who he was talking to. "That is grace," she said aloud, smiling at the thought of how many women his fear would keep him from contacting in the future.

THE NUMBERS GAME

When the Regional Meetings began the following week, the Bleeper was in top form. He welcomed his "team" and mouthed all the age-old jokes about his overbearing wife and other sexist stories. Jessica couldn't have wished for more from him. The impact on the listening women was immediate and fully recognizable. They yawned, shook their heads, then began to compare notes with the other tellers from other branches.

Regional meetings were held in each of the five sections of the bank's territory, usually made up of five or six branch offices. With twenty-nine branch offices, Mr. Talcott set aside an entire week for the early morning regional breakfasts. This quarterly routine gave Talcott a captive audience for his fatherly performance. He led the festivities that followed a very early breakfast. The show included his opening remarks (jokes and all), a report that told how well each branch was doing compared to the others, some perfunctory awards for high achievers (usually a corsage of flowers that the recipient was obliged to wear throughout the day), and the marketing department's dog-and-pony show.

Jessica's part in the show was billed as "the entertainment". Actually, through the years, she was getting to be pretty clever at giving the tellers something to look forward to amid the stuffy statistics and windy speech-making. But the grind of arising early, traveling, and spending so much time in the company of the Bleeper put a damper on her spirit. By the Friday performance, she usually was completely worn out.

This time was different. During the speeches, Jessica could hear the tellers whispering. "I got more than thirty new tickets for the Alices in one day!" "Yeah, well I think I have the record for one hour — eleven." "That's great, but our branch holds the record for one day over all the other branches." "Really, how many?" "I'm not saying until we improve it." "Touchy, aren't we?"

If the Bleeper could have heard this competitive whispering just under the surface, he would have known just what a really great team the bank had. Too bad it wasn't on his side.

The big news came from Central Branch, Terri's office, on Friday. In less than a week, one of the tellers — all by herself — had collected a total of one hundred proxies. Jessica had heard the rumors about this terrific effort, but couldn't find out who it was until the last regional breakfast.

Terri rushed up to Jessica immediately after Talcott delivered his closing joke, one of his more disgusting tirades. He had hit a new low in his contempt for women, and Jessica was almost embarrassed for him. She remembered, however, the effect his words were having on her team players.

The good news Terri brought was just what Jessica needed. "That one-hundred teller? Guess who?" Terri asked.

"I don't know. Gloria? She's always breaking records."

"I'll tell you, but hold onto your hat. It's Debbie! You remember how much she was against us? She tried several times to see Talcott; and when he wouldn't see her, she got mad. Don't you love it? Now she wants to help us."

"I love it," echoed Jessica." Just think, 100-Proxy-Debbie came through!"

By the close of the regional meetings, the leaves had dropped from the trees and Talcott had left for his annual trip to Washington, DC. Once a year, just before Thanksgiving, he went to the nation's capital to make contact with the Congressional delegation and make his voice heard in national politics. It was his own way to sound important.

Once he was invited to address the House Ways and Means Committee, at the time just before deregulation, and you'd have thought he had been invited to dinner at the White House. For months afterward, he'd bring that visit into conversations, often with ludicrous results. Rubbing shoulders with our nation's power people was exactly what Mr. Talcott enjoyed most.

How often had he tried to get himself included in political fund raising dinners with DC dignitaries when they came west on tour. Jessica particularly enjoyed hearing how Talcott, a Republican, eagerly bought a ticket to a $1000-a-plate dinner with Jimmy Carter. And then Talcott's disappointment when a crisis kept Mr. Carter from appearing.

Talcott had been gone about two days when Jessica counted a simple majority in the number of necessary proxies. "We made it!" she shouted as she ran into Operations. "We made it, Sheila," she sang as she waved the numbers under Sheila's nose.

"I always knew you would," Sheila said matter-of-factly, although both women recognized the pretense.

"Let's have a celebration lunch today," Jessica proposed. "I'll make reservations and get our team together — noon at The Poolroom."

Regardless of its name, The Poolroom was considered a classy restaurant, one these women couldn't afford often. Today, however, was a celebration, and nothing would do but the best. Ann and Donna entered the restaurant together and found Jessica sitting with the Alices Operations Department at a large corner table, a wine glass at each place setting.

"This is an occasion," offered Jessica, raising her glass. Reluctantly, the others followed. "Rules are made to be broken, especially when they interfere with progress. As long as we're busting rules, this is a good place to start." The "rule" she referred to was the one Talcott emphasized often: *there will be no drinking of alcoholic beverages during working hours. If you drink during lunch, you are not to return to your desk — and, of course, you'll not be paid for the day.*

Jessica and the others knew of at least one poor soul who had been fired as a direct result of breaking that rule. But, what the heck, the reason for these women meeting today was enough to get any one of them, or all of them, fired anyway.

The lunch that followed also broke all the rules of dieting, which most of the women usually observed. To top off the festivity, there was a killer chocolate mousse. It was a lunch they wouldn't soon forget.

"Numbers, Donna. That's the name of the game, you said. And at last, we have the numbers." Jessica raised her glass. "The Alices now hold a clear majority of the savings account proxies needed to make a vote count at the annual meeting."

"That's good news, Jess, but I would feel a heck of a lot better if we had them all — you know, at least ninety percent." Donna sounded apprehensive.

"Patience, my dear Corporate Secretary," Jessica answered confidently. "We will have them by meeting time. We have a majority now; we're in. Or almost in," she declared triumphantly.

Sheila had been silently enjoying the lunch, but now she came to life. "What are you going to do with your votes, now that you have them?" she asked quietly.

"Oh, well, yeah," Jessica paused, looking around the table, then back to Sheila. "Well, the purpose of getting the proxies, of course, is to elect our candidate to the Board of Directors."

"All very well and good, but who is your candidate?" Sheila repeated.

"Who? Who! Yeah, we have the votes, but who will be our candidate?" With their attention drawn toward getting the numbers, they hadn't given this a thought. Who? They looked at each other around the table. Jessica considered each woman.

Sheila? She didn't think this project was possible and she wasn't supporting it. She was content to remain loyal to the people in power and draw her steam from them. Sheila was loyal, would not cross over... unless she came to see some kind of power in this group of women. And that didn't appear likely with her retirement closing in.

Donna? Donna wanted no part of power. She was content to sit next to it, contribute to it, admire it, but she didn't want to deal with it.

Winnie? Winnie didn't have her own priorities in order. How would she be able to work convincingly with an otherwise all-male board? She might be tempted to seduce them for their votes.

Judy? Poor little Judy was overwhelmed with the power of force. She still maintained that knowledge was power, but when it got right down to it, all her knowledge couldn't stand up to brute force. Judy's power came not from that force, but from her own weakness as a victim.

Terri? Terri was too much of a manipulator. If it worked, do it. She was too close to the new upwardly mobile corporate people who played their roles pretty much by ear. Whatever works!

Me? Definitely no. I'll be the power behind the power if necessary, the mover and shaker behind the throne. But I don't want to sit out front and get hit, not yet.

"Who?" Jessica repeated the question out loud. "Anybody here want to offer a suggestion?" she asked feebly. But there was no response.

"Okay then, that's our next piece of business, our next challenge. It seems to be one that we women face often lately," she began. "I know in my life I have yelled and screamed for power or authority in one form or another, then when I got it, I wasn't sure what to do with it."

"I know the feeling, Jessica," Judy said leaning forward. "I yelled and screamed until Hank let me go back to work after the kids were born. But then I was faced with the decision of what kind of work. Maybe if we thought more about what we want the responsibility for, we would know better how to handle it if we get it."

"*When* we get it," Jessica corrected.

"You did right with your decision, Judy, but this is a bit different." Winnie was speaking slowly. "I guess it's like me looking for a new marriage. If I come close to it I realize it isn't exactly what I want. Maybe I would be happier with a place of responsibility like this, but I'm not honestly sure I could handle it."

"That's a lot of bunk," Jessica cut in firmly. "Any one of us could handle a spot on the Board. Any one of us could make the kinds of decisions that have to be made. What's more, they would probably be better decisions because we would put some of our gut feelings into them instead of denying feelings, as I suspect those guys do!"

"Yes, but men do have a certain capability for making decisions in business that challenge us to do as well." Donna knew she was half-way right, but she also knew as soon as she spoke that the half-way wrong was her own misconception of strength. So she added, "Women are certainly capable. We just haven't had the opportunity."

"That's for sure," Jessica was re-checking her assessments. "How about you, Donna? You have all the know-how, the status, and Talcott might not object to your sitting on the Board as much as he would one of us."

"He's going to object to any woman," Donna said quietly, adding, "and I'm not sure I like that last remark." Everyone knew she was teasing, but there was an edge to it that put Jessica on guard.

"You know what I mean, Donna. You have worked for him a long time. He trusts you. He knows you have the bank's future at heart."

"Just so, I'm not sure it is what *I* want. I'll have to think about this. Anyway, we don't have to decide today, do we? We're having such a good time just enjoying our victory — even if I did wish the margin was just a little wider."

"Donna's right, this is a special occasion, let's not muck it up with details of a future that looks pretty rosy at this moment."

Details, thought Jessica. Such a little bitty detail like answering that almighty question "What do I want?" Maybe that's where we all ought to begin. Because, as the sign says, *If we don't know where we're going, how the heck will we know when we get there?*

Why do we find such difficulty knowing what we want? Jessica seemed to sense what others wanted, or thought she did. If she had listened carefully to herself, she'd have known what it was she really wanted before Dan closed himself out as an option. But she wasn't that perceptive just yet. As soon as she had decided *who* it was she wanted, the question had been changed to *how*.

Jessica passed out breath mints to all the wine imbibers as the group of lunching businesswomen left The Poolhall. They returned to their offices feeling very guilty, a bit heady, and just a tad smug.

The question remained: now that they had the *tickets,* who would be the star player for the Alices?

Not With My Job You Don't

With the mid-point of proxy-raising under their belts, the Alices contingency got their boldest stroke underway — the mailing that went out with the pre-Christmas premium program. All that was required was the smallish proxy card and a note to the shareholder: If you haven't signed a proxy card within the last two months, please sign the enclosed card, date it, and return to…" the anonymous post office address inscribed underneath.

This was about the time that Mr. Talcott finished his trip to Washington and returned to Capital City for a few days bank catch-up before his end-of-year vacation in Arizona.

Rising interest rates, movement of low-cost to high-cost savings instruments, a shift by greedy contractors in housing from single-family homes to condominiums and high-rise apartments all contributed to Talcott's preoccupation with generalities instead of specifics at Stateside Bank. He obviously was not tuned into the goings on at the home office, which gave Jessica a feeling of relief. She knew he would be gone again in a couple days.

His trips were a kind of office joke, but not to his administrative staff. No matter where Talcott was in the world, he kept up his morning routine. No matter what time it was at his end of the telephone, the man called his office at nine every morning to get an update. Every officer had to be ready to jump into the conference room and answer questions on any kind of project — they never knew which project their boss would be focused on at any given time. Ann would pick up the phone and listen to his orders for information, then relay them on paper to Donna, who stood nearby to summon the executives.

"Get Reynolds in here from Loan Servicing to discuss current variable rate mortgages," Talcott would command. Ann would write: *Reynolds, re: VRMs.* Donna would forward the message from another phone.

As they waited, Ann would read off the mail, giving him the senders' names until he'd hear one that he wanted read to him. Then she would open the envelope and start to read. Usually he'd cut her off after a few words with, "Oh yes, I know what he wants, never mind."

As soon as Reynolds had arrived, along with anyone else who had been summoned, Ann would breathe easier and turn over the phone to Donna, who would call each officer to the phone as Talcott dictated. Occasionally, Donna turned on the speaker phone and the officers would hold their regular morning meeting via AT&T. Usually, in less than an hour, the meeting concluded and the phone would be returned to Ann for the sign-off. The chief enjoyed that part most because Ann would ask questions about Mrs. Talcott and how their trip was going, and what sights they were seeing and how hot it was. Then, with a crisp, "Talk to you tomorrow," he'd return to his vacation or his meetings or whatever else he did on those jaunts.

Jessica wondered why they bothered to breathe sighs of relief when he went away. He was just as much a presence when he was in DC or in Arizona as he was in the next office, just as much a pain in th….

Sheila had other concerns the day of his respite in the home office. During his last call from DC two days earlier, he had suggested that she add another staff position to her department. He also seemed to have a suggestion for someone to fill it. Today, Talcott was back with his candidate in tow, and Sheila had been invited — summoned — to sit in on the interview. All she knew about the prospect was that he was a friend of Mr. Talcott and that he was a candidate for the new job in her department.

"Come on in, Sheila," Talcott greeted her. "I want you to meet Jim Hardesty, aide to Congressman Blaine in Washington, DC, at least for another few weeks," he explained. "Jim Hardesty, this is Sheila McDowell, Operations Vice President.

"Happy to meet you, Miss McDowell." Jim accepted Sheila's handshake and politely waited for her to be seated.

"I've heard a lot about you, Jim," Sheila started cautiously, then stopped. She didn't want to carry the conversation. This was the boss's show.

"Jim is working for a lame duck Congressman since the election," Talcott began. "He's looking for a spot to work back here in his home town. Better yet, he wants to work for us. He has an idea that could bring us a substantial increase in capital income. Why don't you explain it, Jim?"

Jim was prepared. He handed a copy of his plan to the president, another copy to Sheila, and he partly read and partly talked from his copy. Sheila watched as he went over the plan. She tried to listen to the words, but something about the expression on his face intrigued her.

The crop of dark hair lay boyishly on his forehead, but the eyes were those of an experienced businessman. Turned down, reading from the pages in his hand, the eyes didn't tell Sheila anything else, just yet. Jim's mouth was speaking deliberately, stressing big numbers, "...two billion dollars annually, with a twelve percent increase each succeeding year."

Sheila tried to guess his age. The plan finished, Jim and Talcott chatted amiably about Jim's future. Sheila's attention returned, and she listened carefully, still analyzing. From the ages of his children and his work experience, she guessed he was in his late-thirties, early forties. He was controlled. *Well, I won't allow the little-boy smile or the easy manner to confuse me.*

This little boy knows his way around! He's slick, she thought. *But the plan he has outlined would be perfect for my department. Wish I had thought of it. Wish I were young enough to have the energy to carry it out. I can use a young man like this. He'd sure make me look good if he can deliver all he's talking about.*

Sheila's attention snapped back to the conversation. Talcott was asking her how she saw Jim fitting into the organization.

"Well, I'd like some time to work this out. Would you want Jim in my department, reporting to me, or would you prefer to have him report to you?" she asked carefully, trying to feel out Talcott's ideas.

As he began to answer, Jim cut in with, "Since we're friends, Tom, I'd just as soon *not* report to you. It might make it easier on Miss McDowell — and you — if I were under her jurisdiction."

"Fine," Talcott responded. "But I'd like to see you eventually have full responsibility for your program. Maybe an equal spot in the department, and report to me through Sheila."

"Well, I wouldn't expect a vice presidency right away," Jim answered modestly, smiling.

Sheila looked directly at him now. *Was he joking? God no.* All traces of boyishness were gone. Still, Jim's eyes eluded her, glancing at random around the room, back to the papers on his lap.

As if a gong had sounded, Sheila realized what was happening.

He wants my job. Maybe not this week, or this year, but he wants my job. Her thoughts raced. This little wheeler-dealer comes in here like some DC hot-shot and is going to use his old friendship and his Washington ties to weasel himself into the organization with this neat con game he's worked up. *Look at me,* she wanted to scream at him. *Look into my eyes, dammit, and say you will be content to work as a subordinate in my department.* But she bit her tongue.

Talcott had turned back to the cost sheet in Jim's outline and was asking questions about starting salary and expenses. Sheila tried to appear cool as they discussed terms.

Hell, she told herself, the salary isn't what he wants. Look at the numbers in that tax-free expense account. Trips to Europe! China! Australia! Nuts! Why is the boss even talking to him?

The answer to that was easy enough. Talcott was impressed with Jim's shoulder-rubbing proximity to Washington power. Hadn't Talcott been one of many willing to pay a thousand bucks to sit in the same room with only the expectation that a President would join them?

"And European money is just as good as Far East or Mid-Eastern," Jim was saying. "At least based on the tax structure. Given the soft domestic bond market, foreign investment is the way of the future — a global future."

The global future. Planning. Outlining. Goals. *Oh, he's a clever one, this guy is,* Sheila thought. One more glance at his eyes and she knew the threat was real. In the near half-hour they had been talking, never once had he looked directly at her.

It was clear, at least to Sheila: *If Talcott hires this weasel, I'm gone.* She was familiar with her boss' ways. He liked new blood and had replaced old with new on many occasions during the years she had been around. "It looks like your turn, old gal," she sighed.

Abruptly, Talcott remembered another appointment, and the meeting ended. They shook hands. Still Hardesty didn't look at Sheila, even as he shook her hand. The woman stood straight, her shoulders back as she left the president's office and headed for Jessica's.

"You want a firm ally, you've got it," she said angrily entering Jessica's office and slamming the door behind her. "That S.O.B. thinks I'm going to lie down and play dead for some flashy kid, he's got another thought coming. I won't let him force me out so he doesn't have to pay my retirement benefits. No sir, no way." She pulled a chair over to the desk and sat down.

"Slow down, Sheila," Jessica moved around her desk and perched on the corner of it while her visitor collected herself, fumbling with her folders. "What's going on?"

Sheila explained the humiliating session she had just been through and concluded with a statement of support for the Alices Project. "I'm with you all the way. I'll even run for the nomination if I have to. That bastard isn't going to cut my career out from under me, not without one hell of a fight. That's the thanks I get for being loyal all through the shit he has handed out for years. That's the thanks I get for sticking around here when others wouldn't. That's the thanks I get...! Well, nuts!" She wanted to use even stronger language, but one of the young vice presidents had just walked in.

"Hey, maybe one of you could tell me what this is."

Jessica's heart sank to the floor. Her stomach with it. In the young man's hand was one of the Alices proxy cards.

"Let's see," Sheila leaned forward. "Oh that. Just one of the new proxy cards we had to send out this year. You know, new regulations. A real pain, but we did it as part of a regular mailing so it wouldn't cost extra. Nothing to be concerned about. It didn't cost the company anything." She moved closer and gently lifted the card from his hand and put it in her folder, out of sight. "Thanks, Bob. I'm in a rush to get all these back as fast as possible."

Convinced of the routine-ness of a matter he didn't pretend to understand, the young man left.

The two women sighed heavily. "Wow, how did that one get out? I thought we had held up mailings to employees?"

"Once in a while one will get through, Murphy's Law or something," quipped Sheila, feeling much better. "At least he isn't smart enough to know what he was holding. Funny how some people will sign anything you put in front of them without questioning or anything."

"You handled that beautifully, Sheila, thanks."

"Nothing to it when you know where your real loyalties lie."

Both women recognized a bond between them now that seemed stronger than anything they had experienced with each other before. "Women together. That's what it's all about," Sheila smiled and left her colleague's office.

Snoops and Rumors

Whether or not anyone else knew it, Winnie always felt pride hearing her voice on the recently installed Automatic Teller Machine hotline. She felt like a star two years ago when she auditioned for the part, repeating the numbers precisely, yet using her sexiest "comforting" voice, "Please replace your card and repeat your account number," or "Please call the Service Department; the number is Five-Five-Five-Oh-Thuree-Nyon-Nyon." She still felt special each time she used an ATM.

Now, as ATM Manager, it was Winnie's job to make sure all the automatic bank machines in all the branches were properly maintained and operating. While making her regular rounds to each of the branch offices, she took the opportunity to pick up whatever new Alices proxies had been turned in. It was during one of those rounds that she heard the first rumor, well, maybe more than a rumor.

"He knows something is up," Terri said, her face pale as her words tumbled out. Winnie had called her first, then phoned Jessica, who hurried over to the Central Branch. "He knows!" Terri wailed as Jessica entered the branch office. "The Snoops were around yesterday afternoon and they heard and they told him." Terri's voice was on the edge of panic.

"Impossible," Jessica tried to sound assured. "He can't know. He isn't even back from his Arizona trip? What makes you think he knows?"

"The Snoops were here. I can tell when they think something is going on!" Terri's eyes looked close to tears.

Everyone knew the Snoops and how they operate. Why Mr. Talcott kept using them, or tried to, was a joke. As soon as one of them walked into an office, everyone clammed up. Still, they worked away in the belief they were getting undercover information for their boss. Jessica had learned a long time ago who they were and how to use them.

Every office has one of these strange office grapevines. Usually some form of code names is used in order to carry out layered conversations that only those intended will catch. Perfectly innocent conversations can be loaded with special information that anyone included will understand. The size and power of Stateside's grapevine spoke loudly about the need for secrecy in that particular organization. It shouted the lack of trust and lack of responsibility that management extended to its employees.

Chief Snoop was Mike Hindemann, an accountant who had been with the company so long nobody remembered what had been his original connection with Talcott. He might even be a relative; no one remembered. He worked in the Personnel Department, computed salaries and withholdings and tax payments, and handled the Bleeper's disgusting job of firing.

Another Snoop was a mortgage department secretary, the girlfriend of one of Talcott's relatives, with a code name of Minor Snoop. Her typing was minimal; her knowledge of the lending business was less than useful; but her snooping capacity made up for the other deficiencies. Some of the staff found it fun to be in the cafeteria when she was having lunch. They would carefully pattern conversations to fill her ears with all kinds of material for her snoop report, things she could mention at the next family get-together, tidbits about this employee and that. She must have been the life-of-the-party with her outrageous stories of strange encounters, dalliances with fictitious people, extraordinary feats of prowess both sexual and athletic.

"Which ones were here, when, and what were they looking for?" Jessica asked.

"Chief Snoop and Minor dropped in yesterday afternoon with some forms for the tellers to fill out, something about medical insurance. I didn't see it. While Chief was getting signatures, he casually mentioned the new proxy forms. Wondered why he hadn't received one since his neighbor had. I told him we were up-dating our files, getting ready for the annual meeting, and his neighbor must have had one missing from the file. He didn't buy it. Said he personally remembered the card on file. I told him I'd look into it."

"And he bought *that*?"

"He seemed to. But Jessica, the question was there. He knows something is going on; I just know he does."

"Okay, but what about Minor?"

"Minor Snoop just kind of nodded and looked like she had swallowed something sour," Terri reported." But then, she always does. Chief Snoop was here when I arrived this morning. He said he had to search some records for signature cards, tax stuff. But while he was working, I checked him out and he was fingering the proxy files and looking closely at the fine print. He took a picture of one on the copy machine and I just know it's going to end up on The Bleeper's desk."

"Okay, that sounds more like a real problem. I'll wander into his office when I get back and see if Mike has any real clues or if he just grabbed the wrong proxy." Then she fairly jumped out of her chair. "What the hell was the new card doing in the regular file?" she yelled at Terri.

"That's what I don't know. Every day as soon as the tellers finish their work, I grab those cards as fast as I can. Maybe this was one that came through the mail. Marge — she's new — handles the mail and she doesn't know about Alice. I wasn't real sure we could trust her, but maybe this would be a good time to find out. Gee, Jessica, do you think they know something?"

"At this point they may suspect, but that's all. Anyway, we figured they might find out, so we'll just keep working and hope we have enough proxies now to continue. The ones we have are all nice and safe and waiting for the annual meeting. Go ahead and talk to Marge. There will be more coming through the mail now, and we have to keep our hands on them. I'll be in touch, and don't worry, Terri. We're getting close; we'll make it."

Jessica wished she felt all that confident as she drove back to her office to track down Winnie. The two met in the hallway next to the copier and Jessica filled in the details of her visit with Terri.

"How many do you think we have now?" Winnie asked. "Can we afford to get careless?"

"Win, don't you worry about a thing. I'll do some counting tonight and see how close we are. I haven't dared to count lately, just kept piling them up and hoping. In the meantime, see what you can find out from Minor Snoop. You two always seem to have things to gossip about."

Jessica wasn't suggesting anything more than Winnie was good at worming out information from a Snoop. Winnie knew it, but gave Jess a crack on the arm anyway. "See if I let you read any more of my diary!" she joked.

"I thought you were getting past that stage," Jessica responded in a serious whisper.

"What do you mean, stage?" Winnie backed up toward the wall facing Jessica.

"You know, Winnie." Jessica felt she had crossed the bounds of friendship and wanted to wisecrack her way out, but she suddenly couldn't think of anything funny, and Winnie was waiting for an explanation. "It's just that women go through stages when they come out of a divorce like yours. The panic of being alone, the search and grabbing at anything male, the frantic feeling of never having another relationship, then the quiet discovery of yourself and the acceptance of a real love. Oh yes, I've been there — and I thought you were getting past the panic-sex stage and moving into real relationships again. The way you talked about your latest friend sounded like you might have found a real person to relate to. That's all I meant."

Winnie knew she should be angry, but she also knew that Jessica was right. "Yeah, well, it didn't work out. I'll tell you all about it when we have time. I better go see what's going on in Personnel."

Jessica watched her walk down the hall and suddenly wished she had left Winnie's personal problems out of the conversation.

Back in her office, she began to clear off her desk for the day. About a half hour later, Winnie appeared at the door, slithered inside with her most conspiratorial slither and closed the door carefully behind her.

"You're not going to believe this." She sounded breathless because she had been holding her breath as she raced along with the news. "The Bleeper has just been on the phone from Arizona, and I was right there and heard what happened. He called Mike in for a speakerphone conversation and I sat there watching it happen. Talcott had Chief Snoop pick up the receiver… for privacy!" She paused to lend full force to her words and let Jessica rise from her chair expectantly before continuing.

"You'll never believe this," she repeated. "The Bleeper thinks Michael K. Hindemann, Senior Vice President in Personnel, is plotting an overthrow!" She sat down stiffly in the chair opposite the desk and waited for Jessica to grasp the implication. Mike was a long-time buddy of Talcott's. He wasn't quite bright enough to make it on his own, so he was content to take the superficial dead-end job at Stateside. He delegated everything to those on his staff and liked to think he *allowed* his boss to do the hiring and firing. Actually, Talcott insisted on retaining the last word on hiring and firing, right down to the last two receptionists. One was fired — by Mike as ordered by Talcott; one was hired — by Mike, as ordered by Talcott. Talcott never did the dirty work himself. Still, he needed control over the staff, which probably accounted for some of the misfits in the organization.

"Mike? but why... how?"

"It's just too incredible! I almost dropped my... well, we won't get into that. He asked Chief Snoop to try to trace the mailing. I guess he got a good look at his neighbor's card after all. He wants Chief to get tough with all the managers working under him and try to implicate them. I didn't hear Talcott's side of the conversation, just the Chief Snoop's, but that's what I concluded from his answers. Mike! Can you believe it?"

Jessica took a deep breath, sat back down in her chair and tried to get her brain to think. The end of the day was a bad time to get hit with something like this. "Let's sleep on this, see what develops tomorrow, keep very closely in touch and then... I'll talk with Sheila first thing in the morning; you talk to Donna and Judy. Maybe they've heard something. I... I... just can't think anymore now."

"Oh Jess, it'll be okay. I'll see you first thing in the morning. Try to sleep tonight; I won't. But then," she grinned, "I have better things to do!" Winnie swayed across the room and turned to wink just as she reached the door.

Two days passed before anything else was mentioned. Sheila was the one to bring the news this time, shortly after the morning phone call from Talcott.

"It's Mike. He's quit," she said slowly.

Jessica's chin dropped. "Why? Did Talcott fire him? What happened?"

"Apparently Talcott gave Chief Snooper Mike the word to find out what he could from the managers, and when they suggested that Mike was planning something, Mike blew up. Mike has been edgy about doing Talcott's dirty work for a long time, ever since he was spending overtime auditing the auditors and running the leg work on that legislative lobbying job. This must have been the last straw."

"How devastating to do all that shit work for the boss, then be accused of disloyalty!" Jessica's words were not lost on Sheila.

"When Mike learned that Talcott was suspicious of his managers, that translated to him that the boss was suspicious of *him,* and that did it. Fifteen years of loyalty and shit-shoveling and The Bleeper practically accuses him of treachery. So he quit!"

"Sheila, what have we done?" Jessica felt the full impact of her part in forcing Mike out of his job. Until then, it had been a kind of game, but now she felt they were tampering with people's lives.

"Probably made a sane man out of Mike and extended his life by ten years or so. Actually he didn't look that upset. In fact, come to think of it, he looked… rescued."

"You're not just saying that?"

"No. Now that I'm thinking about it, he looked rescued, liberated. Incidentally, Jess, Talcott is on his way back. As soon as that receiver went down he must have been re-dialing. I took the call and he said he was coming in tonight, cutting his vacation short."

"Where does that put us now?" Jessica was still gasping. "Are we clear?"

"That's the funny part. Isn't it weird how Talcott immediately suspected the managers, the men, of conspiring, not the women. I don't think he even considered us for one single moment. It never occurred to him that the women of his organization would not be anything but true-blue."

"Ooh, poor pun. But are we clear?"

"That's the bad news. Since Talcott didn't think I knew anything about the proxies, he casually mentioned that we'll have to get out a new mailing for new proxies, right away. He wants all the staff to come in Saturday and get started. Of course I told him we already had a Saturday session scheduled, you know, the new interest rate adjustments that have to be double-checked."

Jessica's brows lifted with her question. "I didn't know anything about a double-check. Something the Auditors dreamed up?"

Sheila grinned. "No, something I dreamed up. If he wants a new mailing to go out, that's my department. But you know, Jess, how busy we are at this time of year, just before the holidays!" She over-emphasized her words and Jessica recognized her meaning. "You won't believe the time it's going to take to get this mailing out!"

Proxy Proxy Who's Got the Proxy?

And it did take time. First there was the holiday season, with Christmas and New Years downtime. Besides normal mail overloads, other obstacles turned up in the Operations Department like a heavy black cloud of poor luck. Machines broke down; the computer printout service arrived days late (and was misplaced for another day); the printer was *slow* delivering new mailing cards (they ran out of stock and had to order from Philadelphia, right in the middle of the holiday mail)! Then addresses got smeared in the mailing machine; a whole load went to the post office without postage (and was returned). The creativity shown by staffers in the entire delaying tactic was one of the best-staged operations any of the Alices Committee had ever witnessed.

A few of Talcott's new proxies got through, were returned to the Operations Department and — would you believe it — lost? A few actually were filed in the official Proxy Committee file, but they were all small accounts, not worth more than a few votes.

The holidays for Jess were a disaster. She couldn't help but remember the year before when she and Dan were full of plans for their future. She had managed a pile of gifts for Amy and Richard and even held a cocktail party for her friends. Without Dan, Christmas just wasn't jolly. She considered calling him once, actually dialed, but hung up when a woman answered. "Didn't waste much time, did he?" she chided herself. I thought he wanted to spend the holidays with his children this year.

She heard from Will that week between Christmas and New Year. "Hi, my darling," he began the conversation. "Did you have a nice Christmas?"

"Who is this," Jessica asked innocently.

"Wha… it's me, Will. You didn't…" but Jessica cut him off.

"What do you want?" she asked briskly. *Why did I pick up the phone? He sounds so lonely. No, no, don't continue to do this to yourself. Drop this bum, this womanizer.* With renewed determination, she lowered her voice and said almost in a whisper, "Will, it's over. Please don't call me again."

She heard only a brief sputter on the line before she hung up. *That does it. Now I don't have anyone. No Will. No Dan. Nobody but me. Well, maybe that's enough.* She turned over and went soundly to sleep.

By January, Talcott seemed to step up his manipulations, this time in the mortgage department. Since there weren't any Alices people (meaning women) in mortgage management, Jessica had no way of knowing about this move until too late.

"He isn't satisfied with the return rate of his proxies and he's going after loan proxies," Jessica told Sheila when they met in the hallway.

"How did you find out?" Sheila asked.

"I happened to be in the copy room when Minor Snoop was running off the letter to mortgage customers. Here's a copy, but keep it low. Nobody seems to know about this; apparently Talcott is playing close to the vest with it."

Sheila slipped the letter inside an open folder and read it. "This is one of his own gems, which means he isn't trusting anyone to read it over for editing. He must really be worried not to let even his secretary see this. Did you ask Ann about Talcott's mailing?"

"Not yet, but I plan to… real innocent-like," Jessica replied with a smile. "Maybe things aren't as bleak as they seemed when I first saw that letter."

But they were. Very bleak. The mortgage files hadn't been counted in the Alices Committee's assessment. After all, they were worth only a single vote apiece, yet there were thousands of them, and it now looked like they might make the difference. Donna had been right to try for ninety percent of available proxies.

The Alices met for lunch on the January Friday ten days before the meeting. Winnie rode to the restaurant with Jessica.

"You're very quiet today, Winnie," Jessica commented gently after a few blocks of driving in silence. "Anything wrong?"

"No, not wrong. In fact, I think something… everything… is very right." Another few blocks of silence, then Winnie continued, "Jess, I'm not dating for a while. I guess it's a New Years resolution, but I haven't had a date since before Christmas. Does that mean I'm celibate?"

Jessica smiled, "No, Winnie, not long enough, I'm afraid, but what happened?"

"I took some time to think during the holidays, and I talked with my daughter a lot, and I decided there wasn't any good reason for my dating just now. I thought I was looking for a new husband, but I guess I was just scared of being alone. Well, being alone isn't so bad, I found out. I got through the holidays, and ever since I have rather enjoyed having the extra time. Don't laugh, but I'm learning to play the guitar with Becka."

"Hey, that's great. I'll bet she loves that."

"Yes, you know, I hadn't realized how much she missed me, or that I missed her. We haven't had time… or rather, we didn't take time… to get used to being on our own." She turned excitedly to face Jessica. "We made plans, Jess. Becka and I sat down and listed all the things we'd like to do together, and we're working on the list. When it gets warmer, we'll bicycle, go on picnics, take little trips. Right now, I'm swimming at the Y-pool with her and we're making music on our guitars."

"Do you still feel empty without a man around?" Jessica asked softly.

After a very long pause, Winnie responded. "No, not empty. I'm not sure I feel empty at all anymore. I have Becka, but… I just realized as I'm saying this… I have me!"

"Welcome to the real world, Winnie." Jessica spoke proudly as she maneuvered the car into a parking space. "I knew you'd make it. You've discovered the magic in you; I knew it was there all along." Only a twinge inside her reminded Jess of the pain left from seeking her own magic after Dan left.

"I'm not saying I won't be looking for a man," Winnie defended, "but now I don't feel like I *need* to. If there's one out there for me, he'll find me. If not, I really don't think I'll feel a great loss." The astonishment was clear in her voice as she recognized a new strength inside herself.

"One more thing, Jessica. Maybe it has to do with this new way I'm feeling about me, but I'm going to use my full name — Winifred — from now on, if you please. Maybe it has to do with feeling more grownup, at last. You know, time to give little Winnie a rest and let Winifred take charge."

Both the women were smiling as they entered the restaurant and shifted their attention back to the business at hand.

The mortgage proxies were beginning to appear in the mail. Donna recognized them as the envelopes were opened in Talcott's office before immediately disappearing.

"I went through his desk last night after he left, searched every place in that office. He probably takes them home in his briefcase and is storing them there," Donna reported.

"Like I do," Jessica scowled and slumped. "Well, we'll just have to hope we have enough. The majority we had at Thanksgiving has fallen. I've been counting, and the number is just about 53,000. With a potential of 77,000 votes in Operations, and 31,000 in mortgage, that means we aren't even at the half-way point if we count them together. Usually we don't bother with those mortgage proxies; nobody figures they're worth the effort to go after them. If they begin to come back in big numbers…" She didn't want to think about that. "Only one more week before the annual meeting. There isn't much we can do now."

Lunch began quietly. The women nibbled listlessly as their heads continued to chew over their plans. Nobody wanted to venture speculation at that moment.

It was Judy who brought up the mention of the Willmar Eight. "They didn't give up," she said quietly. "The hung on for two years, facing freezing cold winters and burning hot summers, derision from their friends and neighbors, loss of their incomes…"

"Yeah, and they still failed. Don't forget how it all ended." This came from Ann. "They lost their jobs and…"

"Hold on," Judy interrupted. "They moved rights for working women ahead by miles. Maybe we still have a long way to go, but at least we're making waves. I'm sure this will make the evening news — at least for a couple nights."

"Good point, Judy," Jessica said. "We're already preparing press releases about our success."

"Maybe we ought to have one to cover our defeat... if that happens," Ann added.

"We need a name — like the Willmar Eight — something to call attention to our purpose, you know, in case of... uh... a defeat." This came from Winnie. "How about the Alices Rebellion? That'd make a good headline."

"I like it." Jess smiled and accepted nods around the table. "Reminds me of... was it Jefferson who said that 'a little rebellion is a good thing'?"

"At least we'd get some press if our plans don't work out," Ann added. "Public pressure might save some of our jobs."

Sheila held her club sandwich, half-eaten, in one hand and waved with the other. "Hey, we can't keep up this doom and gloom. We still have a week to go; maybe he'll get careless with those mortgage proxies and we can grab a few and... er... lose them. It looks rather dark right now, but we still have a chance. Maybe we better do some planning about what we'll do when we make it!"

Whatever eating had been going on suddenly stopped. Teeth paused in mid-chew and all eyes went to Sheila.

"Make it?" Ann stared at Sheila.

Not since last fall had the women taken any time to consider this question. They had wavered in volunteering themselves to sit on Talcott's Board of Directors, so they had left the entire matter up in the air. Maybe if they didn't talk about it, the problem would solve itself.

"Yes, what if we make it? What are we going to do?" Judy repeated.

Jessica was pleased — and surprised — that it was Judy who seemed eager to find a strand of hope. "You're right, Judy. We need to decide that pretty soon. What if we make it? Who are we going to elect to the Board? What are we going to do with our votes?"

Maybe the early part of lunch was quiet and subdued, but the last part was close to boisterous. The women talked excitedly about the joy of winning, the look on Talcott's face, the expected reaction of their co-workers, their own thrill of achievement. Their plans ran toward the outlandish in their enthusiasm; an onlooker wouldn't have believed they were serious. Perhaps they weren't. Perhaps they didn't believe they would make it. Jessica compared their wild ideas to those she hears from people who talk about winning the lottery.

Some of the ideas included: We'll move women up the ladder, into the mortgage department, into positions of decision-making. We'll tie Talcott's hands when it comes to railroading his ideas through the Board. No more will he find it easy to steamroll over his directors like a dictator. We'll suggest some of the older Board members retire. We'll look closely at salaries and equate women's take-home with men's. We'll set some guidelines for addressing all employees with respect in the future. We'll move more women into top management.

But which woman? Who will we elect? The sobering question remained unanswered.

Jessica wanted to get serious. "Actually, there ought to be two nominations, to replace the two oldest members of the Board — those who are over seventy-five. They haven't really functioned in years; they sleep through most meetings and are constantly on the phone to ask me what happened to this resolution and that. Would we dare hope for two?"

"Why not?" Winifred was excited. "Certainly there are two women in or around the organization who could sit on the Board."

Sheila tapped her water glass and ceremoniously asked for the floor. "I nominate Donna to sit on the Board of Directors," she said.

"I couldn't, Sheila. I'm employed with the company. Directors have to be non-employees."

"Where does it say that? Read your by-laws," Jessica shot back. "Look at Talcott. Doesn't he sit on the Board? Isn't he an employee?"

"I never thought about that," Donna returned. "He always tells me that Board members are supposed to come from outside."

"Of course he does, Donna. He doesn't want any employees around to see what goes on. This way he's got more control over what the Board does." Sheila repeated her motion which was seconded by Terri, and they all put their heads together to think of a second nomination.

Somebody from outside. Somebody who would do them some good, and somebody the Board could learn to accept. Most of them already knew Donna and had worked with her. They'd accept her as part of the Board, if they had to. After all, the Alices Committee wasn't trying to sabotage the Board, just even things up.

"Do you all remember when Marvin Parker died a couple years ago?" Sheila asked after a few moments. "Marv had been one of the bank officers, one of those good-natured people who genuinely are missed when they leave their jobs or die. Marv had been appraising some property one afternoon, suffered a heart attack, and just keeled over. His wife Janet has been coming around asking my advice about investing his estate funds. In the past year she earned a real estate license and is doing very well in her business. She specializes in investment property and has brought the bank a lot of business. Do you suppose she would agree to sit on the Board? Or would you want her?"

"Yes, and yes," Jessica said. "What a wonderful idea. She would make a good Board member. How do the rest of you feel?"

"She sounds like a winner," Judy offered. "I've seen her in the office and she has come back to life in the last few months. Marv's death totally wiped her out, but she's coming along fine."

"I hear she has a boyfriend," Winifred added. "Sure, she sounds like a winner. I'll vote for Janet Parker."

Around the table, all agreed that Janet would make an excellent choice, if she would accept. When the vote came to Donna, she was near to tears. "You don't know how happy this makes me. Janet will be excellent, but she also will be wonderful to work with. If I'm going to be fed to that Board as its first woman member, I'd sure like Janet along to share the fun."

Jessica and Judy visited Janet that afternoon and found a very happy, confused, willing candidate for member of the Stateside Board of Directors. Janet thought the whole idea was exciting and challenging, although probably not feasible. After lengthy explanations about the whole Alices Project, Janet agreed that if things got as far as putting the women's committee in control, she would accept the election to the Board.

There's something different about you today, Judy," Jessica noted when they got back in the car. "Something has happened. You sound different, more constrained."

"I'm glad it shows. Lets me know I'm doing the right thing."

A long pause followed, then Judy continued, speaking in a very low voice, painful with remembering. "Hank and I had another battle over the holidays, violent, frightening… for me and for the boys."

"You don't need to go over the details, Judy."

"No, that's okay. It helps to talk about it. I don't have anyone else to talk to." She paused again, took a deep breath, then continued. "He'd been drinking, as usual, and… we argued about some little thing, what to eat for dinner or something, and he started in on me again. The words. The terrible, hurtful words, how I was no good at doing anything, how he had to make all the decisions, how I never followed his orders, all jumbled and out of reason. He just got angrier and angrier and then… he threw a beer bottle at Jeremy…" Judy stopped for a moment, then quietly, "It could have killed him. Jess, he could have killed our child."

Jessica pulled the car into a small parking lot and turned off the motor. The two women sat silently for a few moments.

As Jessica began, "Judy, you have to get out…" Judy interrupted with, "I did. I did, Jess. I packed up the boys' things and what I could of mine and I left. More than two weeks ago. I've been living at a shelter for battered women since before New Years. There seemed to be a chance for a clean new start at the beginning at the new year, and I took it."

"How is Hank taking this?" Jessica asked.

"I'm not sure. I left when he was out of the house. He doesn't know where we're staying. I phoned and told him we were all right and he was so apologetic. Jess, he cried over the phone. The people at The House told me to expect it, and I realized how often he had done this before. I just told him it was too late to be sorry. I'm gone — for good."

"What now, Judy?"

"I don't know. That's the hard part. I get so angry that I'm tempted to go back and face him down. Let him know I won't put up with his bullying anymore. I'm scared too, really terrified of facing him. Yet, that house is as much mine as his — more in fact. I've been making the payments from my paycheck… everything's a real mess, I just don't know what I'll do."

"You've done the hard part, Judy, the leaving. Making that decision and doing it, that's the hard part."

"But, what now? I can't stay at the shelter forever. I need a place to live, for the boys. Oh, maybe I ought to go back."

"That's up to you, but listen to your words, 'go back'. You've started doing something for yourself. Think hard before you decide to 'go back'."

"I was hoping you'd say that." Judy nearly smiled. "It would be easier if somebody had told me what to do, made my decision for me, but you're right. I have to take over now. I have to make my own decisions. I sorta know what I have to do and I'll do it, but it won't be easy."

"The good stuff never is. But it *is* worthwhile. And furthermore, you have some good friends to lean on — all the Alices, to start."

Now Judy did smile. "Thanks, Jess. I'll remember that. The good stuff isn't always easy."

Jessica took Judy's hand and patted reassurance into it. Then she started the car and they continued driving back toward the main office.

Donna had spent the afternoon working out the wording for the nominations to be presented to the Board at the annual meeting. She also wrote out the agenda the Alices group had suggested for consideration at the newly elected Board's first meeting: really-equal-pay for all officers of equal rank and tenure, really-equal pay for all branch managers (whether male or female), really-equal pay and career opportunity for all tellers and applicants (when a male showed up in the teller line, he was usually moved out for management training and more pay), and raises for all tellers.

And she wrote a brief speech that included: *The all-male Board doesn't realize that women today work for the same reasons men do, with the same skills that men have, and therefore, deserve to be paid according to their jobs rather than their gender. The all-male Board also is out of touch with what tellers do. They need to know how valuable are the people on the front line of action who deal directly with the customers and their financial needs. While the Board insists on mentioning valued customers in every news release, it somehow keeps offering them the lowest-paid employees to handle their accounts.*

When she was finished with her re-writes for nominations and "little changes" to be introduced at the annual meeting, Donna sat back and smiled to herself. She was trying to think what it would be like at the meeting.

She even dreamed further, and wondered what it would be like in the Board Room with two women sitting at the table instead of serving coffee. She was beginning to actually enjoy this feeling of… what was it?… power? Yes, power. Donna realized that she could do whatever had to be done to pull this off. What's more, now she knew not only that she *could*, but that she *would* do whatever it took.

The very idea of holding that power gave her a heady feeling, heady and pleasant. Damn, maybe now they'll listen to my ideas, my opinions. Opinions, yes, I have my own. I never used to, always depending on others, men, for my opinions. Now, they'll want *my* opinions, and I'll give them. Nice thought, expressing my own opinions, my very own. Powerful concept.

"What's more," she spoke to the empty room. "I may hire a male secretary for this department."

Maybe that's going too far, she thought as she walked to the copy room. *After all, we still aren't sure if we have enough proxies to get the nominations to the floor.* Donna was smiling, however, as she made copies of her work, placed them carefully in her briefcase and left for the weekend.

Yes, a male secretary for the department.

Black Friday

During the following week — the week before the annual meeting — each of the members of the Alices Committee worked with fingers and toes crossed and breath held at "pause". They walked slowly, cautiously, quietly. And they avoided Talcott's office as if it were an alien planet.

Talcott, sure that his managers were moving to push him out of office, held his daily meetings and loaded all the (male) managers with impossible tasks. He had them preparing reports and charts for the annual meeting, outlining proposals for new projects, making infinite surveys and providing infinite statistics, ostensibly for use at the annual meeting. He hadn't shared his suspicions, and used Mike's departure as the reason for considering major reorganization plans for the bank.

Talcott was busy watching the managers; the managers were busy carrying out his unreasonable demands; and the Alices Committee was busy collecting proxies and planning the annual meeting's unexpected agenda. Reorganization indeed!

Logistics of the final move were prepared as carefully as any other plan ever envisioned. Donna had prepared two sets of scripts for the directors. Jessica had arranged for the proxies to be delivered at the appropriate time. Sheila, as the lone female manager, was prepared to inform the managers at the last minute to expect some fireworks.

One for the money, two for the show, three to get ready and… it all seemed in line and ready to go.

Until Friday — Black Friday.

The early morning started with the usual officers' meeting. There were a few clues that should have caught somebody's attention, but everyone was too occupied with their own thoughts, worries, and concerns, to notice. Most apparent should have been Talcott's suit. He was wearing black that day. In the past, the record showed that whenever The Bleeper came dressed in black, somebody got fired. The second portent was the relative calm of the meeting. No Christians had been sacrificed that morning.

Immediately after the meeting, Talcott summoned Sheila to his office to discuss the proxy votes next Tuesday. Sheila needed support and asked to bring Jessica, to report on the advertising plan that printed the official notifications of the meeting. It was a stretch, but Talcott agreed.

"Good morning, ladies," he greeted them, believing he was being gracious. Since it was past ten o'clock, he offered them coffee. They declined. They needed both hands free of distractions to handle whatever was going to happen.

"I'm going to share a secret with you two," he said in a low, conspiratorial voice. He paused to let his words sink in. He would have liked a reaction, but they sat straight-faced, waiting. "Some or all of my managers are trying to take over the bank and they're planning to do it at the annual meeting."

"No," said Sheila in amazement.

"No," said Jessica with disbelief.

"Yes," said Talcott. "I haven't been able to find out who; they really have their clues hidden from me and they're doing a great job of lying to my face; but I'll be ready."

Why had he chosen these two women to confide in? Jessica was swallowing hard, but she managed to ask, "How? I mean, how will you stop them if you don't know what they're doing?"

"That's why I called you two here this morning. I want you to stand at the door of the theater next Tuesday and keep out anybody who isn't cleared by me ahead of time. I also want you to have two of our best people seated across the aisle from the managers to signal me if any of them makes a move to approach the stage. If that happens, I'll just announce a postponement of the rest of the meeting. They aren't going to get away with this."

Jessica and Sheila were straining not to look at each other. If Talcott hadn't been preoccupied, he might have noticed that the two women barely moved.

"Wouldn't they work from the inside?" Sheila asked, and almost immediately regretted it.

"Inside? What do you mean inside?"

"Well, er, I'm not sure, sir, but I'd think someone making a move like this would have someone inside to help them. I mean, they'd need to get into the theater, on the stage, or at least down front…" She wished she hadn't started.

"You're right. I wonder if any of the Board has been contacted. I'll have to put them on the alert too. Thought maybe there wouldn't be a need to bother them with my suspicions, but maybe they know something. Hadn't thought of that. Thanks, Sheila."

Jessica wanted to change the subject fast. "Is that all you want us to do? Keep guard at the door?"

But Talcott was on another channel. "Must call the Board. They've got to be looking for something strange in the agenda notes."

He pulled his private phone out of the desk drawer and began to dial his Board members. Sheila and Jessica slowly stood up, motioned their departure, and walked out.

"Sorry, Jessica," Sheila started to apologize.

"No need, I'm not sure if this is good or bad. I just wish he'd have some other fire to put out today. All we need is a couple more days and we're home free…"

"…or dead," Sheila finished the sentence.

The women were headed toward the elevator when they heard Talcott's voice booming behind them. "Hey you two, get back in here."

They froze. Something in his voice sounded ominous. Had the first director he called told him something they didn't want him to know?

Talcott was holding the receiver to his ear when they re-entered the office, talking to someone in whispery tones. "Well, let me know if you sense anything is wrong. And let me know if you hear anything. All right, Nate, see you Tuesday."

He turned toward the women as he hung up the receiver. "I forgot to tell you the most important information. It might help you feel more at ease about the stability of the bank."

"Oh?" came the weak reply.

"Yes, after I heard about the takeover, I got busy and started getting new proxy votes. You remember, just before Christmas when we mailed them out? Well, I put the pressure on the mortgage department to get returned proxies from them, and I have a bundle. I mean, they came in like we've never had mortgage proxies before. I must have about eighty percent mortgage proxies and I think our savings proxies are up to about seventy-five percent now. I had them mailed to my home rather than come through here, just as a precaution. I'm going to have the last word at that meeting Tuesday, whether or not those guys make a move!"

Jessica's stomach did a fast turn. She didn't remember how she got out of that office. Sheila must have taken her arm and steered her, but she was feeling numb herself as they again started toward the elevator.

"Sheila," she moaned. "Sheila, we're finished. I had no idea he had sidetracked those things away from us. Oh damn, damn, and double-damn! What will we do? Oh damn!"

They rode down the elevator in silence, not sure whether to cry or cuss or both. They looked like stones walking toward Jessica's office. Judy noticed and followed them.

"Hey, guys, what's wrong?" she asked when they got inside. "You look like you've seen a ghost."

"Not a ghost. A demon, a monster, a vampire!" Jessica answered.

"We've had some very bad news," Sheila began to explain. Slowly, she voiced the words that wanted to stay in her throat: "Talcott claims he has a big majority of proxies tucked into his portfolio. He's been having them sent to his home and he's been concentrating on mortgage proxies. Says he has a majority… big majority."

Silence.

Then, "Have you seen any of his cards?" It was Judy speaking. "Have you seen what he sent out? I mean, maybe he didn't word them right, or they're dated wrong, or he's made some other major mistake. After all, if Donna didn't have anything to do with them, he could have really goofed up."

It was a light, but not a bright one, and the women couldn't have felt more dejected.

"Let's find out. Let's get hold of one of these cards and check it out. After all..."

"Give it up, Judy. We're finished," said Jessica. Not usually one to throw in a towel, she had been keyed up for so long, had fought down disillusion so many times, had kept up a cheery front so often that she didn't have any reserves. "We're finished," she said, staring straight ahead at nothing.

Sheila and Judy left her sitting behind her desk, shaking her head, staring.

By early afternoon, the members of the Alices Committee had all heard the news. Terri at Central Branch heard it from Judy who had dropped by the bank's downtown branch after lunch. Some kind of joke, she suggested to Judy. "I feel too confident to let it get to me now. We've been going along so well."

"It's true, Terri, but personally, I don't think we're finished yet. That's why I'm here."

"I'm calling a TGIF party." Terri ignored her friend as she dialed Jessica's number.

"Let's have one last celebration," she suggested joyfully to Jessica. "Let's meet across the street and have a celebration drink after work."

"Oh Terri," wailed Jessica. "You haven't heard..."

"Yes I have," she answered. "Judy's right here. She told me, but I don't believe it. I think we're all tired and scared and plain worn out, and I think we need our spirits lifted. Besides, even if we lose this one, look at what has happened to us as individuals. How about it?"

"What have we got to lose?" Jessica responded with a half-smile. She knew what was at stake, but she couldn't think of any reason not to get together one more time. Jessica made the calls inviting the committee to the after hours party. *Who knew what would happen after next Tuesday? We may all be in jail or mental institutions by then.*

Never mind next Tuesday, no one could have predicted what would happen there — that day — that black, black Friday at the Central Branch.

A little man called Buddy changed the tone of doom and gloom into utter chaos about mid-way through the afternoon.

Banks are excellent targets for holdups on Friday afternoons. Tellers are busy, cash drawers are full, and thieves know it. Tellers, trained in security and defense, are instructed to follow directions of holdup threats, avoid confrontation, and protect the customers and themselves, whatever the dollar loss. "It's only money," they are told. Thieves know that too.

Buddy chose Stateside Bank's Central Branch that Friday afternoon, about two-thirty. He walked inside and stepped into line. At the counter, he held his hand inside his jacket menacingly as he told the teller to empty her cash drawer into the bag he pushed toward her. The teller was Debbie, the Alices' former troublemaker. And, while Buddy didn't know it, she had hit the silent alarm about the same time he reached into his jacket.

He might have gotten away with the heist except that Terri and Judy were standing in the center of the lobby at the same time. Terri's trained eyes roamed the teller line as they talked, and took notice of Debbie waiting on "a customer" with her head down for a very long time. Tellers are encouraged to look at their customers as they work.

Terri shifted a bit to get a better view of "the customer" and saw that Buddy's hand was inside his jacket.

"Quiet, Judy," she whispered. "We have a holdup going on," and she moved very slowly toward Buddy.

The lobby was filled with customers, dutifully waiting behind the corded signs that read, "Wait Here For Next Teller". Terri wasn't thinking; she just recognized a man was about to take something from her domain and her brain flashed red. Angrily, she took a deep breath, then stepped quickly directly behind Buddy, pushing him against the teller window, pinning his arm. In her fury, she whispered angrily, "Drop it. Drop it, damn you, or I'll mash your head in." She was holding him so tightly, in fact, the gun couldn't drop, although he had let go in surprise.

It felt to Terri like she stood pressing Buddy against the counter for hours until the police arrived. Then it was over. Buddy had been carted off; the bank was closed for the day; the funds were safe; Debbie and Terri had been taken to an inner office by federal investigators; and the corporate office had been notified of the attempted holdup.

"No need to send anyone over," Terri had told Talcott. "The feds are here and everyone is safe." She believed the strength in her tone of voice for the first time. She had handled a dangerous situation in what she considered a level-headed way, and she felt strong.

But Talcott wasn't pleased. "That was a stupid thing to do, Missy. The man was armed. You know the rules — no confrontation. You're just a girl! He could have killed you and half the customers."

In a way he was right; it could have turned out otherwise, but Terri had trusted her own instincts, sized up the situation, and acted as she felt necessary. In a way, she had set up her own rules to play that day's game. Apparently, Buddy had only his own game plan; her rules confused him. Funny how that worked.

"I had the drop on him." Terri talked to Talcott like a grade B-movie. "The bum never had a chance." The adrenalin still pumping, Terri obviously enjoyed teasing her boss. She sensed, however, that he didn't see the joke. He was still having trouble getting past a mere woman overpowering an armed man.

When the calls were finished, the feds gone, the reports filed, it was time to send everyone home. Business hours had ended hours earlier.

It was then Terri and Judy remembered the party. Would the Alices still be there? Had they heard of the holdup?

"Come on, Debbie, you earned a party. Would you like to join us?"

At the tiny bar across the street, Sheila had brought the news of the Central Branch holdup. "Everyone is all right. I imagine Terri and Judy will be along soon."

"This indeed may go down in history as our Black Friday," Jessica began. "Other things have happened as well. This morning

Talcott let us know he has a large majority of proxy votes from the cards he sent out before Christmas. We didn't think he had that much, but we must have figured wrong, or we didn't figure he'd know how to pull this off without anyone knowing. Sure, he suspects the managers, but he'll get some clues on Tuesday when none of them makes a move to challenge his proxies. Even Old Bleeper can figure that out."

"But he still doesn't know about us. We could just sit tight and say nothing, couldn't we?" asked Winifred.

Silently, the women sipped their drinks. They were dissolved in a gloom that held them close together, like they were wrapped in a cloak of it. Sheila and Jessica saw only piles and piles of proxy cards — not theirs.

Their gloom was interrupted by the arrival of Terri, Judy, and Debbie. The trio was greeted with hugs and pats on the back for their bravery. "It was really Terri," Judy explained. "You should have seen her. I'll bet old Buddy will tell his friends in the pen about this super-strong woman who ruined his holdup."

"I'll bet nobody hears about it, not from good old Buddy. I should think he wouldn't want *anybody* to know he had been taken down by a woman," Terri answered. "By the time the story gets to the pen, I'll have turned into some big hairy bruiser with a machine gun in my pocket."

"You're probably right, Terri," said Debbie-the-teller. "But I for one am very happy you took him. He made me so mad with his thinking that he could just walk up and take my money. I'll bet he wouldn't have bothered if I had been a man. I wonder if there would be fewer bank robberies if tellers were men."

"Don't worry, Deb, it'll never happen," Terri told her. "But it *would* be interesting to wonder if men tellers would bring out women robbers."

"Now you're getting silly," Donna put in. She had seen tellers after a holdup and these women weren't following the pattern. They were too glib, too calm. They had been through a serious jolt to their emotions and here they sat sipping drinks and telling jokes.

"So here's to our success," Winifred said, raising her glass for a toast. "Here's to our overwhelming The Bleeper and his old proxy cards." (She never gave up.)

"Why not?" Sheila returned.

"And to Terri and Judy for foiling the robber."

"Cheers," they all added — those brave women named Jessica, Sheila, Winifred, Donna, Judy, Terri, Ann, and... even skeptical Debbie.

After a few moments, Terri and Judy looked at each other. "We've had our workout for the day," Terri began, "and things turned out all right. This will turn out okay too, you'll see. We just need some time to relax."

Judy had been very quiet during the toasts. Now, as they gathered their jackets and purses to leave, she could hold back no longer.

"It isn't right! It isn't right that men think they can use their muscles to make us do what they want. It isn't right," she spoke softly but intensely. "This afternoon when that awful man stood facing Debbie with a gun, I could see Hank holding a gun on me. Or the kids. I had to get away. I had to get them away from him before he did something awful to us. That's when I left him. It's time you all know. I'm living in a shelter with the children and waiting... waiting... I'm not sure what for. All I know is that I never want to feel that bad again. I don't want to hurt anymore." Tears streamed from her eyes as the words tumbled out.

They all listened quietly as Judy continued. "Hank would bang into the house, slamming doors and waking the children. He'd yell for something to eat and expect me to jump. He twisted my arms, punched me, slapped me around like I was an old doll of some kind, some *thing* without feelings, without a brain. He didn't even care that the children were watching while he slammed me around.

"He was so cold; I couldn't reason with him; he didn't listen to anything I said. He accused me of running around — and I was there all the time. I hated to go home. I hated him; I hate him. Why are some men so cruel? Why do they take their hate out on us? At first he used just words, awful words, calling me awful names and accusing me of awful things. Then the hitting started. Once he used one of the kids' bats. He hit my knees so hard I could barely walk. I don't know him when he gets that way." Judy was shaking as she remembered.

After a moment, she looked up and quietly asked, "What is it that makes men so full of hate and so angry at the world? So angry at the people who love them? When I saw that man today, I saw Hank. Oh god, what's wrong with me? What did I do wrong?" Judy continued to sob.

"Nothing, Judy. Absolutely nothing. You did nothing wrong. Hank was wrong. He had no right to talk to you like he did or hit you." Terri comforted her friend. "You have to know that it wasn't you."

"Old Buddy really did me a favor," Judy shivered as she gulped out the words.

"Everything will be just fine," Terri added, her arm around her companion. "You did me a favor too just now. You... you..." and the young woman's voice rose in anger. "You should have killed him. I should have killed him. I feel right now like I'd like to kill somebody. It isn't fair." She spit out the words. "These damn men have been pushing us around for too long and I for one am not going to take it any more. I'll get me a gun. Yes, that's what I'll do. I'll get me a gun and I'll carry it and the next time one of those animals comes close to me I'll blow his head off and I won't even feel bad. I won't cry. I don't cry anymore about the unfairness of men having everything, doing everything, being everything while we women just clean up after them.

"It isn't fair and I'll have my time, I know. I'll have my time. Next time I'll be in charge and the Buddys of this world will learn to leave us alone. I'm so damned tired of taking their crap all the time and not being able to fight back. It makes me feel so helpless, so damned helpless." Then Terri too began to sob, quietly, immersed in her own anger.

Terri's companions sat with their arms around her and each other. They felt their own fears and rage as Terri and Judy were feeling theirs for the first time. Whatever would happen next, these women had been through enough to show themselves they could handle whatever came along. Whatever happened.

From Monday's Ashes...

When Terri entered the Monday morning staff meeting, she had acquired a worn, tired appearance. She and Judy found each other and compared notes of their weekend.

"I really came apart in the middle of the night," Terri said. "I woke up screaming inside, my whole body pouring out sweat. I shook so hard my husband thought I was suffering from a fever."

"Yeah," said Judy. "I woke up suddenly and saw the whole picture again, that awful man, you racing toward him, the gun. Oh god, the gun looked like a cannon."

"You know, I never saw the gun. I hadn't realized that. I just felt that god-awful fellow and smelled the grease on his hair. He really was short, you know." The two women smiled and wondered how long the flashbacks would occur.

Judy sat through the meeting without taking a single note. When she noticed this, Jessica was sure something was wrong. She watched her friend closely, and discovered Judy wasn't even paying attention. Her head was somewhere far away. No small wonder, thought Jessica.

"Let's get this meeting finished," Talcott finally bellowed. "We're wasting time here when we should be getting ready for tomorrow's annual meeting. Let's hear the reports from all the department heads. Is everything ready?"

Jessica listened as each vice president intoned his report, repeating the numbers that Talcott certainly had already engraved inside his head. "Do you have that on a chart?" Talcott asked each manager. "Jessica, be sure they are framed and in place tomorrow at the theater."

"Yes sir," Jessica responded, nodding every time Talcott talked in her direction.

When Talcott stood to deliver his closing remarks, Jessica allowed her eyes to rove around the table. The vice presidents in their dark navy jackets sat starchly upright in their chairs. Donna gazed intently at The Bleeper as he spoke; Sheila diligently kept her notes; Winifred was looking at the wall opposite her chair, her thoughts elsewhere, perhaps with Judy.

As for Jessica, she had resigned herself to allow the inevitable to happen. If The Bleeper had the proxy majority, she'd just have to dust off her resume and follow up on one of those help wanted ads she noticed in Sunday's newspaper. She knew the consequences when they began this venture so many months ago. Now time was running out, and it was almost time to face the music. Tomorrow would tell. Do or die. Make or break. She realized she had never felt this way before, risking everything on one chance. It was a heady thought.

As the meeting concluded, the managers left the room, briskly, as if they were escaping from a cage. Jessica worked her way over to Judy. "Hey, Jude, what's on your mind?" she asked lightly. "Everything okay?"

"Yes, I think so. You know, Jessica, I can't help but feel there might be something about Talcott's proxies that may still make ours legal. I just wish I could get my hands on one. Do you have any ideas?"

"Let me think. Maybe Sheila could. But The Bleeper is hanging onto his cards like they were gold. They are, I guess."

"Well, see if you can find me one, just one," Judy repeated, then waved and headed down the hall.

A pink stack of phone messages lay on Jessica's desk when she entered her office. The day before the annual meeting always brought one crisis after another. She ruffled through the stack: photographer about the new ads, print shop, framer having trouble putting the Retirement Funds Report in a frame to match the others.

Mike Hindemann! Wonder what he wants, she thought. *Call him at home*, it says.

She had dialed his number and was continuing to sift through the messages when Dan's name popped out at her. "Call Dan at home", the note said. Her home? Chicago? What did "home" mean? And why now? She hadn't heard from him since… how long ago was that? It seemed like years.

With no answer from Mike's phone, she clicked the receiver and absentmindedly re-dialed — her own home number. Three rings, then, "Hello," it was Dan's voice.

"Dan? What… what are you doing here?" sputtered Jessica. "What on earth are you doing here?"

"Just thought you might need a strong shoulder to lean on," he answered. She could hear his smile in his voice.

"Oh, you're right there. But why… how did you manage? I thought this was production week for the magazine. How'd you get away?" Jessica's mind raced at the idea of Dan back in her life. Had he really left?

"I'll explain when I see you. How about lunch?"

"I can't," Jessica answered. "Sorry, but I can't take the time today. I have a stack of emergencies piling up and I just wouldn't feel right…"

"I only make the offer once," Dan cut in. "Come on, you deserve a break, even a short one. I'll meet you over at The Poolroom at twelve-thirty. You'll be back at your desk by one."

"Well, you twisted my arm. I'll go along, but what… how… why…?"

"All will be clear, but I have to see you face to face to explain."

Jessica closed her door and began to sort her other calls. She tried Mike's number again, wondering why he had contacted her.

"Hi Mike, Jessica Nadeau returning your call. What's up?"

"That's what I'd like to know. Jess, I've worked with you a long time and I trust you to tell me what the devil is going on down there."

"Going on? What do you mean?" Jess began to tap her pencil anxiously.

"I keep hearing about takeovers and in-house plotting. The old man fired me because he thought I was at the bottom of it. I'm not. I wasn't. But I'm betting that you know who is. Maybe I'd better tell you that I've been sleeping soundly nights and enjoying my days like I haven't done for a dozen years. Jessica, you can't know how relieved I was when I quit. Hell, I'm not even looking for another job yet. I feel too good and I'm afraid of getting into another corner like Talcott put me in."

Jess didn't know whether to console Mike or congratulate him. "I envy you, Mike. You're out of here. Those of us who remain are going through our own kind of hell right now. He's got the managers chasing each other. He's looking for treachery in every one of us. And I'm up to my ears getting ready for tomorrow's meeting."

"That's why I called. I'm sure there'll be some fireworks and I wouldn't want to miss it. You're in charge of the door, aren't you? Or has he changed everything around?"

"Yes, I'll be in charge of the door." Could she trust Mike not to betray her, tell The Bleeper she let in an outsider? "But hey, Mike, you haven't closed your account at Stateside yet, have you?"

"No."

"Well then, you're still a customer. You're a bona fide shareholder, and there's no reason you can't be there."

"Except that Talcott wouldn't be too thrilled to see me."

"He won't. I mean, he doesn't have to see you. You know how busy he is on Annual Meeting Day. Wear a blue suit and melt into the background. Don't worry, Mike. If you want to come, I'll keep you out of his clutches." Jess grinned at the thought. After all, Mike had been a kind of sacrifice. He deserves to be in on the meeting, whatever happens.

"I'll arrive late. I'll let the Board get seated before I come in. See you tomorrow, Jess, and thanks."

"No bother, Mike. I'll look for you tomorrow."

The remainder of the morning disappeared. By noon the crisis pile had disappeared and Jessica left her office with an almost-clear desk.

Donna entered the elevator just behind Jessica and the two found themselves alone, able to talk freely. "Thought you'd like to know Judy thinks she has hold of one of the Bleeper's proxies. She's going to bring it over this afternoon so we can comb through it for loopholes."

"One loophole; anything, Donna. I'd settle for one itty bitty loophole. Thanks for telling me, but somehow, I don't feel much better."

"Where are you going?"

"Lunch — with Dan. I guess I forgot to tell you. He flew in this morning from Chicago, for lunch!" Jessica smiled at her understatement.

"Sounds wonderful. Did he have a reason? Or just loneliness?"

"I'm going to find out now," Jessica called as the elevator door opened and she dashed off.

Dan stood just inside the restaurant door and slid his arm around Jessica's waist as she entered. "Hi, gorgeous," he whispered as he planted a kiss on her cheek. Jessica could feel her world slip back into place.

"Hey, this is great. You look great. The whole world looks great at this moment, and just because of you. Did you have a good flight?" She even surprised herself at her feelings of relief and joy at seeing her friend, no, much more than friend. At this moment he seemed more like *partner* than *friend*.

They chose a table at a window overlooking the water, a peaceful view of mid-winter calm, lazy waves beating time on the pilings. They both ordered seafood salads and sipped at their wine as they watched each other's eyes for clues. "Sure you won't get into trouble with your boss over the wine?" Dan asked.

"Frankly, my dear, I don't give a damn. If I'm going to be hung for a crime, it might as well be a whopper. How's that for priorities? I consider breaking the wine rule a bigger crime than overthrowing the corporate government."

"Is that what you're doing, really?"

"Well, isn't it? We're defying the structure, the corporate organization, the *roools*." She strung out the last word and made a face.

"Actually, I'm not sure everyone would see it that way. You do, because you're so close. But if an article reported this on the front of the *Wall Street Journal,* it would carry a headline more like 'Corporate Board Challenged By Well-organized Takeover Bid'."

"I'd rather see 'Women Triumphant in Corporate Board Purge'." Jessica looked closely at Dan. Why was he here? Why had he come all this way? Without a word of warning to her? Silence for all these weeks and now he just shows up like nothing has happened. For whatever reason, I'm glad he's here. I miss having someone to bounce off my work problems. I miss him. I'll just enjoy this, she thought, and see where it goes.

Dan bit off a corner of a Parker House roll and asked, "How much press do you have lined up for tomorrow?"

"Don't talk with your mouth full," Jessica scolded, adding, "we sent out the usual releases. But I've told you how nobody ever covers these things."

"Maybe tomorrow would be different if you alerted someone that there might be fireworks. Win or lose, you could use the press, couldn't you?"

"Hmmm. Maybe you're right. I think I'll call a couple business news editors and hint at something happening. Thanks. If we don't make our proxy numbers, at least we'll let people know we were trying. That alone might be worth losing our jobs..." and then a second thought, "...or permanently being blacklisted in the banking world."

"I don't know. If I were an employer, I think I'd like to have gutsy women like you and your committee to commandeer my business and make it go. Whether or not you women realize it, the risks you all are taking are rather commonplace in the male business world. How do you think I got my job? Somebody quietly bought up shares of the publishing business and ousted the owners by sheer numbers. It happens all the time."

"Sure, in the male world. Why do there have to be two business worlds, like we were coming from different planets or something? What a dynamic business would emerge from a coalition of gutsy women and risking men, all directed toward the same goals!"

"Maybe someday, Jess. And maybe because of you and your Alices."

After a pause to eat, the two sat back and looked out over the bay. Warm sunshine in the middle of winter always felt so much warmer inside through a window than it was outdoors. Gulls with nothing more important to do swooped with the wind currents.

Dan quietly reached over the table to grasp Jessica's hand. "Jess, I came here not only to offer moral support, but I've reached some conclusions. First I have to ask about the guy you were entertaining New Years Eve."

"What guy? I didn't… Why do you ask that?"

"I called to wish you a happy New Year. Some guy answered. I thought…"

"Jessica smiled. "I spent the evening with my children, Dan. I remember now, the phone rang and Richard answered. He said that nobody was on the line. Was that you?"

"Boy, have I got egg on my face. I guess his voice has changed. I've been worse than miserable since then thinking you were…"

"Well then, as long as we're clearing things up. How about the woman who answered *your* phone when I called, the day after Christmas?"

"You called? It must have been Danielle. The kids spent the holidays with me. There certainly weren't any strange women in my apartment; you can be sure of that." A pause, then, "You called me? Oh Jess, these last weeks have been holy hell for me."

Jessica was holding her breath. Dan seemed so serious.

"Jess, I've been miserable. I miss you, terribly. I need you." Just the words Jessica had wanted to hear but believed she wouldn't. She smiled at him, encouraging more. "I want to be with you all the time, not just on sporadic trips or over the phone. I want us to live together…"

"Yes, Dan, I do too, but you know the problems."

"Don't interrupt. I want us to live together wherever you would be most comfortable. I feel strong enough about my skills and my experience to secure a job anywhere, even here. I've been thinking about starting a business of my own, and I can do that anyplace, geographically. What do you say? Is it time to make us legal?"

"Dan, oh Dan," all she could say was his name. Her heart pounded like a teenager in love as she recognized all the emotions she had been packing away for a someday. "Dan, I've been miserable without you. I missed seeing you, talking with you, holding you. There must be some way we can work this out."

"I'm willing to try. Do you think we need a mediator?"

"Get serious, idiot. We're two grownups. We can find our own way."

"I believe that. I believe we belong together and believing that, I know we'll find a way."

The two sat in the January sunshine gazing into each other's faces.

"We do belong together," Jess said after a moment. "I've thought about backup plans in case everything falls through tomorrow. I've been checking out the market for opportunities in advertising. I've even toyed with the idea of my own company. I think I could make a go of it. I have all the connections, and I could specialize in financial marketing and serve companies with a small staff and large client lists."

"You know, Jess, our jobs aren't all that different. In fact, they kind of dovetail, me writing, you advertising. Did you ever think about publishing our own magazine? I'm just talking off the top of my head, but out loud that doesn't sound half bad."

"The prospect is challenging, I admit. After tomorrow I may be willing to take on anything even remotely challenging. After tomorrow, either I am ready to conquer the rest of the world, or I'll be daring enough not to care about safety nets. Let's wait and see… tomorrow… then decide."

"A deal," Dan squeezed her hand, tossed down his napkin carelessly, and pushed back his chair. "Half-hour's up. I promised I'd get you back. See you after work?"

Jessica's answer was a kiss on his cheek. "You bet!"

The pair walked hand-in-hand out of the restaurant and back to the office building across the street. Tomorrow! It didn't seem such a menacing thought anymore. In fact, Jessica was actually looking forward to Annual Meeting Day for the first time in years.

ANOTHER ANNUAL MEETING DAY

About mid-morning the following day, Jessica went through her Annual Shareholders' Day routine. She arrived at the theater by floating on clouds. Dan had stayed with her the night before, and they talked well into the night.

Sure they could get along with each other, but what about their children? Yes, she depended on her job, but that might be gone in a few hours. And yes, Dan was happy in Chicago, but he'd sure consider following his heart into the sunset for his Jessica.

The important part was that they were talking, discussing a future together, and loving each other again.

Jessica crossed the stage, noting the dusty curtains, recalling the previous year's annual meeting and reveling over how much had happened since. She was forcing herself to keep her spirits up. Dan's support was keeping things in perspective, but she had a fleeting thought that this might be her last annual meeting. She wondered if she felt better or worse for that thought.

Displays were arranged, the microphones checked. Then Jessica moved to sort the name-signs for the Board members. "The old fools," she muttered as she straightened the signs, making sure the names on the meeting agendas (scripts) matched. "Someday, you old goats, someday somebody will be strong enough and smart enough to move you out and move in some younger, smarter people, preferably women. Or is that redundant?" she smiled to herself. "Smarter, women… yes, redundant. We have to assume that women are smarter, at least more flexible, more open…"

Her thoughts were interrupted by a sound at the back of the theater. Peering into the half-darkness, she could sense someone was there, but couldn't see who.

"Who's there?" she called.

"Just me," came back Dan's voice. "Thought you might need some company."

"Dan!" she called out as she hurried down the stage steps. "I didn't expect you to be here. You're about four hours too early if you're here for the meeting."

"Naw, I just didn't have anything else to do. And I missed you. Are you alone?"

"Yes, this is my job, nobody else wants it. Did I tell you that we think we've found a loophole in Talcott's proxies?"

"No, what's the deal?"

"Let's get out of here. I have to get back to the office and make a few calls before the meeting. I took your idea and put bugs in the ears of the city newspapers and all the local media. There may be a good representative press here this afternoon, and how Mr. Talcott hates reporters. And guess whose job it is to make sure who gets in and who stays out of the meeting?"

"You don't say. I'm not one of your shareholders. Will I have trouble getting in?"

"Of course you're a shareholder." Jess sounded surprised he didn't know. "Your name is on our joint savings account. You knew that. And that makes you a shareholder, with about eighteen votes, I think at present."

"I'm impressed," Dan joked. "Well, in that case, I'll be here to vote my own shares if you think that will make a difference."

"It might, who knows?" At this point Jessica wasn't going to turn down anybody's backing.

She and Dan left the theater and walked the few blocks back to her office. He left her at the elevator and took off to find a sandwich. Jessica didn't feel hungry, just excited, anxious, scared, elated, and shaky.

She phoned Terri, who was heading the group of tellers that had boxed all the Alices Committee proxies. Their job was to transport them to the theater and keep them in a van in the parking lot until the right time.

Jessica found Sheila in her office working out the wording for her interruptive speech that would challenge the Board's proxy committee. "Maybe I ought to just stand up and say, 'Just a darn minute, boys'," she joked. "At least it would be honest."

Passing Ann's desk, Jessica got a high sign that Talcott was occupied, "going over his speech and covering all exits, so to speak," his secretary told her. She stuck her head in Donna's office, but nobody was there. She couldn't find Judy at her desk either.

Winifred breezed past in the hall as Jessica stuck a note to Judy's calendar. "Hi, Jess," she called from the doorway. "What's up?"

"I'm not sure, Winnie… Winifred," she answered. "Do you know where Judy and Donna are?"

"The last time I saw them they were headed over to accounting. I think Donna was going to re-count the number of possible votes, last minute."

"Good, I'm going to return a couple of phone calls, grab a cup of coffee, and get back to the theater. Gee, I hope things go all right this afternoon. Do you have a backup plan, just in case, Winifred?"

"You know me, I bounce well. Anyway, I'm not worried. You know, Jessica, the most important thing to come out of this experience is the way I feel about myself, well actually, the way we all feel about ourselves. Do you realize how much we've grown in the past year, as women, as individuals? At least I have, and I know Judy has, and Donna, even Sheila."

"And Terri and Ann and '100-Proxy-Debbie'," Jessica added. "It's the next year that is frightening right now. Think how much all of us can grow if we pull this off!"

With that thought swirling in their heads, the two gave each other a quick hug for good luck, and went to carry out their own parts in the drama that was to come.

Lights, Cameras, Action

As usual, The Bleeper was preoccupied with himself and his appearance prior to the meeting. He also was concerned about security. As soon as he arrived at the theater, he combed his hair, then checked all the doors to be sure they were locked, all except the front entrance where he met Jessica.

"Be sure you stay right at this door, Helen," he warned. "Nobody is welcome today except our own people."

"Yessir," she responded. She already had spotted two newspaper reporters, but since they had the sense to come dressed in blue, Talcott didn't notice.

Sheila at her station next to the coffee and cookies smiled as she waved at her friend and her boss. Talcott saw nothing incongruous about one of his vice presidents serving the snacks. "We've been through a few of these, haven't we, Helen." Talcott did small talk badly.

"Yessir, we have," Jessica responded. "This is my sixth."

"Naw," he said in disbelief. "That long? Well, this one may be different, if those guys try anything. We'll be ready. I have my ace in the hole."

"Oh, what's that, Mr. Talcott?" Jessica asked innocently.

"I have it, that's all. You'll find out in time," Talcott grunted, and walked off to greet a real, live shareholder who had just walked in.

He must be referring to his proxies, Jessica hoped. But as the man says, we'll all find out in time.

Meetings at Stateside generally started right on time. That day was no different. The sleepy old Board members, the executives, managers, supervisors, and tellers from around the branch system were all in place as Thomas Talcott Jr. made his grand entrance, marching majestically down the aisle and up the steps to the stage.

"Call the meeting to order," he spoke in a monotone as he ceremoniously pounded the gavel on the old table. The houselights dimmed and spotlights hit the stage. The show had begun.

Jessica waved Mike in at the last minute before she and Sheila closed the doors. They quietly moved down the now half-darkened aisles, Jessica on the left, Sheila on the right. Both took their seats across the aisles that framed the middle block.

The familiar blue wave showed darker in the front, where the top executives sat, all the way to the back where the light blue uniforms of the tellers completed the wave.

Jessica still couldn't locate Judy. Donna had shown up just before the meeting started and had preceded Mr. Talcott down the aisle. They hadn't had a chance to talk, but Jessica couldn't miss the smile on Donna's face. Terri sat with her teller troop toward the back where they could make an easy exit at the proper time to bring in the proxies.

And seated in the special area reserved for shareholders was Janet Parker, dressed in a stunning turquoise suit, her hair freshly cut and styled. Not only would she be a responsible addition to the Board, she would be photogenic too.

While there were no cameras evident in the audience (Talcott would not allow cameras or reporters if he knew), Jessica was certain a camera or two was stashed handily somewhere close by. She certainly knew about the four reporters who showed up and now sat among the shareholders.

And there was Mike Hindemann, former executive officer, now sitting with the twenty-seven shareholders. Had word of possible fireworks drawn that many of them to the meeting?

Talcott began to read from his prepared script, the routine opening remarks, the roll call accounting for the presence of all the Board members. As each was introduced, they nodded acknowledgment, then paged randomly through the scripts in front of them. While the president continued with a few ad lib remarks, the Board appeared confused as they tried to find their places.

Talcott continued following the script relentlessly. He looked a bit restless, probably unsure for the first time about what lay ahead. How often had he warned staff that he didn't like surprises.

Perhaps he had given them the weapon they would use today. Well, he had decided he wasn't going to be surprised at anything. He had found them out and had taken counteractions. Tight control, tight security, keep the ship tight, he thought. He didn't consider the resulting "up-tightness" that was generated in his employees.

The speech was underway. The bank's Board President Talcott fingered his copy of the script as he continued to read about "the forward-moving company" and its activities over the past year. He was in the midst of discussing the two new branches under construction when he became aware of the stir at the back door, about the same time Jessica did. She heard the pause in his speech and turned her head to look. Talcott squinted through the spotlight to see what was happening.

Both Talcott and Jessica saw Judy enter the door at the back of her aisle with two television reporters carrying lights and video cameras in full operation. Simultaneously, a third reporter and TV camera entered the other aisle door. They approached the stage slowly, to record the scene for the night's six o'clock news.

Talcott continued his speech, torn between the loss of secrecy and his enjoyment of having cameras trained on him. If this hadn't been such an important meeting… but he *had* to continue. The next part concerned prospects for the coming fiscal year.

Judy slid into the seat next to Jessica and poked her ribs. "I think we have them," she whispered, "enough proxies of our own to counter his. Donna had a chance to look at a few of Talcott's proxies and you know what? He forgot to leave a line for the date. If the signer didn't date it, we should still have the operative date. Just in case, we have contacted a few of the large account shareholders who should be arriving shortly to override their written proxies."

"My, my, you have been busy, Judy." Jessica was breathless.

Across the room, Donna took notice of Judy's arrival. They caught each other's glance and nodded understanding. As Corporate Secretary, Donna was seated in the front row taking minutes. Board members Anderson and Owens already were dozing at the Board table as Talcott droned on, only slightly more agitated under the glare of camera lights.

The room had just quieted down following the arrival of the TV crews when another disturbance at the back door gave Talcott reason to pause. This time, eight tellers tried to slip quietly into the theater carrying large boxes. They placed them in the aisles adjacent to the first row of tellers, then slipped back out the door, returning a few moments later with more.

Jessica needn't have wondered if Talcott knew what was in the boxes. He did. As the door opened quietly the third time, he paled in the hot lights of the cameras. All his blood must have drained into his shoes, because his face turned as white as the script he let drop to the table. *My god,* he thought, *they've got them. They've got proxies by the ton.* But how? when? and the biggest, most frightening question, why? *Never, never in my twenty-eight years at the head of this business, never has anyone questioned my authority. What is going on?* he wanted to know.

At the same time he didn't want to know. If there hadn't been shareholders in the audience, and the cameras… god, the cameras… he had to keep going. *Heads will roll, you can be sure,* he thought. *I'll fire them all, every last manager, every last one of them. They're all in it and they're all history, gone.*

He continued his speech as best he could. After all, the cameras would run this part on the evening news. What could be more important in today's meeting than the plans for the upcoming years?

Talcott slightly rushed the speech to its conclusion, then asked for the next item on the agenda.

"Election of officers, sir," Donna answered politely. "The Proxy Committee is asked for its report."

Jessica grabbed Judy's hand and the Alices Committee held its collective breath. Later they told each other they couldn't remember breathing for at least seven minutes.

The Proxy Committee chair, old Mr. Owens, was helped to his feet and droned out the report, written in front of him. It seemed obvious he had no inclination that anything was amiss.

As he finished, Sheila stood up slowly and called to Mr. Talcott. "Mr. Chair," using her best inclusive language. "Mr. Chair, may I address the Proxy Chair?" she asked, continuing without waiting for a reply. "If it please the Board, I challenge the Proxy Committee to show its votes and wish to present sufficient votes showing election of a new proxy committee."

"Preposterous!" Talcott said, turning from pale pink to red. "Sheila? What's going on?" Dazed, he fielded the interruption, nodded at Sheila, then ceremoniously asked someone offstage to pull open the drapes behind the Board.

As the drapes opened, the audience could see stacks of boxes, which Sheila realized were Talcott's contribution to the proxy fight. And he was smiling, this tyrant who thought he could steamroll his way through life. Well, he'd find out. Sheila turned and asked, "Judy?"

Judy stood slowly. With the ceremony to match Talcott's, she asked that the Proxy Committee review the proxies in the boxes on stage. "I think you'll find, sir," she spoke confidently and carefully, "that those cards carry no date and are therefore invalid. The television cameras continued to whir, recording the entire action.

The Bleeper just stood there. He couldn't answer, he couldn't move. Talcott had turned from red to livid. How dare someone challenge his committee, his proxies? How did Judy get in on this? Where did she see any of his precious cards? And Sheila, why the hell Sheila? What did she have to do with this? Where was Mike? Talcott had expected Mike to lead whatever happened. And here stood Judy and Sheila! What were they saying? What was happening that he couldn't make sense of? What was this strange turn of events?

But Talcott knew his "Rules of Order" and he numbly asked for a vote count by his Proxy Committee. They would have to sort this out. Three Board members, fully awake now, moved to carry out the order.

"If you please, Mr. Chair," Sheila insisted, "we would like a neutral vote-count committee named from the floor. Perhaps from the shareholders present. And we request a review of the proxies on stage as well as the proxies presented by the Alices Proxy Committee."

"What the hell is the Alices Proxy Committee?" Talcott almost sputtered as his mouth moved to do as he was told and his brain rebelled with every available cell. Who does she think she is to tell me how to conduct this meeting? Shareholders indeed. Was this all planned? Is that why there are so many shareholders here today? No, that old broad couldn't have brought this off… she must be speaking for the other vice presidents.

The count committee was named: Mr. Owens, the chair of the Board's proxy committee; Sheila, representing the APC. and three shareholders carefully chosen from the audience, two that Talcott knew commanded control of a few thousand shares themselves. He'd show Sheila who was running things. The new counting committee moved to a table quickly set up in the orchestra pit just below the stage.

Talcott watched in disbelief as the one hundred-fifty-plus tellers moved their boxes forward, one by one — like offerings to an idol, a cause — some tellers returning for seconds. Terri had wisely promised each teller she would take part in this ceremony. That way they'd protect themselves against being singled out for punishment. In other words, they were ready. If one went, they all went.

The boxes were crammed with the distinctive proxy cards of the Alices Committee, collected dutifully by the tellers. In the last month as tellers realized the importance of the cards they had been collecting, they had exerted the extra effort it took to be sure the numbers would be there. They wanted to be part of this event, and here they were with their contributions.

The counting continued under Sheila's leadership, for nearly two hours, but nobody noticed the time; nobody left the theater. The cameras had been turned off when the counting started, and laid carefully on the floor of the hastily designated "press area". Reporters from time to time approached Talcott for a statement, but he continued to mutter, "Plead the Fifth," in his confusion instead of "No comment," which he usually used.

Jessica took advantage of the counting break to distribute her press release to the media reporters who waited for the outcome. The release began, "Whether or not the Alices Rebellion is successful…" and ended with a brief review of progress in the women's movement for equality in the workplace.

Mr. Talcott watched the counting, barely moving in his chair on stage. He slumped from time to time, but his eyes never left the counting table. Donna was monitoring the counting process. *At least she could be depended upon to be on his side.* He wasn't sure about the shareholders and the old goof who chaired the Board Proxy Committee.

Then he lost Donna. It was she who pulled down box after box and extracted samples of Talcott's new proxies. "No, sir, sorry," she shrugged her shoulders in mock despair. "There are no dates on any of these cards. I'm afraid they are all ineligible for counting."

The pro-tem committee entered into its work with gusto. They quickly set up a system, and moved along rapidly, sifting the proxy cards and placing them into neat stacks. After the first hour, the Board's proxy chair could see the trend and pulled away from the table, leaving the counting to more nimble fingers.

The suspense grew. If time were a factor, Jessica might have estimated the actual time at two or three times as long as it took. Whenever she was sure there weren't going to be enough Alices proxies, another box would be poured onto the table for verification. Slowly, neat rows of authenticated proxies began to pile up, and about three-fifty p.m. the last box was opened, the numbers were tallied, and by four-thirty, the results were final.

When Sheila handed her the numbers, Donna couldn't believe it, yet she could. The smile that passed between them was clearly one of success. The numbers were there; the tellers had been thorough; all was in order.

Donna walked slowly up the stairs to the Board table and presented Talcott with the tally sheet. There was no other way to go. He had to pronounce the Alices Committee in full authority. He didn't know how it had happened; he had been beaten.

The television cameras were turned back on and Talcott read the names of the Alices Proxy Committee handed to him by Sheila. Good god, he thought as his eyes skimmed the list. Aloud he fairly shouted, "My god, they're all girls!" And the cameras recorded.

He looked helplessly at Donna. "Women, Mr. Talcott, women," she said, smiling. He knew then he was alone. He read the list, barely audible past the third row (but picked up clearly on the camera sound tracks): "Jessica Nadeau (he even pronounced it right), Sheila McDowell, Winifred Flemming (Winnie? Really?), Judy Robertson, Donna Westerhoff, Terri Litton-Clark, and Ann Emerson." (*Who's Ann Emerson?* he wondered.)

As the last name sounded, the cheering began. The Alices Committee stood up, everyone hugging everyone, tellers jumping up and down, tears all over the place, smiles and various noises of joy. They had done it! They had actually pulled off their dream. The cameras recorded the moment, a moment that would stay with these women forever, something to tell their granddaughters, who probably would shake their heads and comment, "So what?" But at that moment the world was new for the women at Stateside Savings.

Mr. Talcott took his time restoring order, and attempted to continue the meeting with the election of officers. Sheila took over and handed out the agenda items that Donna had carefully prepared. The Bleeper choked out the nominations of Donna Westerhoff and Janet Parker to the Board of Directors and announced the election results, again to the cameras. He had lost two seats on the Board, two seats he previously had firmly controlled. And now he had gained two girls, two *women* he definitely could not control.

The meeting ended quickly after the election. Talcott could see no need to attempt any more business that day. In fact, he doubted he ever would be able to achieve anything on behalf of his bank again. Maybe he had come to the end of his value to Stateside. Maybe he ought to liquidate his shares and bow out. After all, he was getting close to the age of retirement.

Yet, he held onto the thought he could manage a way to counter this ridiculous turn of events. Maybe he could get out of this one yet.

That Tuesday evening he went home to a cold, delayed dinner and a long, sleepless night.

THE BEGINNING

The victory party for the Alices Committee was held where it had begun, in the posh Pacific Lounge. They took over the entire restaurant and signed the bill as a State Savings Bank expense. After all, they had two members of the Board in their party. Jessica had watched the boss sign off such bills with even less of a reason; she learned well.

The committee members had made hurried calls to spouses, lovers, children, parents and friends, all of whom arrived with smiles on their faces. The shareholders at this extraordinary meeting spread the word and brought entire parties with them to celebrate. A couple members of the news teams stuck around, hoping to add color to their eleven o'clock news reports. (Only the local stations were in time to get the story on the air at six o'clock.) And the tellers were all invited to be the special guests at this bash.

While champagne was served and the partyers were toasting themselves, the restaurant turned out a superb buffet. After today the committee would have to watch the budget more closely because of its new responsibilities, but this evening no one much worried about budgets. Mr. Talcott would pick up this tab and they were enjoying themselves.

As the dessert crumbs were being finished off, Donna brought out the agenda items she wished to present to the new Board of Directors. Seated at a kind of head table, members of the newly formed Alices Advisory Committee followed their copies:

Item 1:   Group teams would be organized to replace the hierarchical bank organization. Jobs would be re-classified to reflect the changes (eliminating vice presidents and assistant vice presidents). Each team would select facilitators to serve terms on a rotating basis. Titles shifted accordingly to indicate the work.

Item 2:	A representative of the tellers would be chosen to serve as a consulting non-voting member of the Board.
Item 3:	A child day-care center would be arranged for bank staff members.
Item 4:	Salaries would be reviewed against comparative worth and equal pay guidelines, with emphasis on work rather than title.
Item 5:	Tellers would include an equal number of men and women who would receive career mentoring.
Item 6:	Additional women would be sought to serve terms on the Board of Directors.

Janet agreed with every item and asked everyone present to help the two new Board members prepare strategies for implementing them during the ensuing Board meetings.

The tellers, extremely pleased with their part and with the outcome, began to discuss the possibility of forming their own negotiating group, a subject never before discussed out loud by Stateside staffers.

The reality of representation on the Board was heady stuff, overwhelming. Chatter up and down the tables continued into the night as employees and officers of Stateside and their friends and families planned their futures.

"What if…" and "what next…" and "why not…" and "we could even…"

Jessica just sat and stared at the scene and muttered, "We did it! We did it!"

THE CLOSING ACT

The power balance had shifted, tipped upside down. At last Stateside Savings Bank was being run from the strength of the most qualified people, the staff. Mr. Talcott had lost his grip on the company by the challenge from "below".

Like many companies in the 1990s, Stateside Bank became an employee-owed bank, efficiently guided by a team made up of department specialists, equally representing both women and men. Team members regularly alternate department representation in order to acquaint them with all working facets of the bank.

The first Board meeting under the new organization clearly indicated what lay ahead for the bank. The two aging directors had been replaced. With the power clearly out of Talcott's clutch, three other directors expressed their interest in the issue of the position of women at Stateside. At least they were open to discussing the agenda that Donna and Janet presented. (Two of the directors were holdovers from a recently merged bank and weren't any too fond of Talcott's tactics from the beginning; the third was a young — fifty-nine-year-old — lawyer who had been retained a year earlier by the bank.) These five — two women and three forward-looking men — were able to carry the votes on most items that opposed the president's manipulations. Theirs was a coalition of spirit that was to steer Stateside through some very rocky months.

The first item on that first meeting agenda was the election of a Managing Officer for the bank. The entire Board agreed that Talcott was a good manager as long as he was properly directed. They voted to keep him on, at least temporarily. They all knew he would be taking his cues from the Board, instead of the other way around.

This was as it should be, something called *democracy*, where majority rules and power goes to the people who do the work instead of to the tyrant at the top. President Jefferson had it right:

> *"A little rebellion now and then is a good thing."*

AN UPDATE OF THE ALICES

The Alices Committee continued as an operating Proxy-Check Committee. Jessica was named facilitator of an autonomous Public Policy Team, which she managed as if it were her own business. She and Dan were married and started their own advertising business on the side. Two years later, Jessica resigned from her bank job when the couple launched their own full-scale company that continues to provide opportunities to live full lives, together. Their children, all grown up, keep in touch through Facebook.

Donna and Janet proved to be the two most responsible members of the Board. They moved comfortably into the Board operations and shared duties easily. Their views sometimes were new to the men who slowly figured out why women had to be considered. After all, most of their customers were women; most of their employees were women. It turned into a very educational process that benefited even the women members of their own families.

Sheila was promoted Senior Team Coordinator, doing the work of the liberated Mike Hindemann. Mike asked to re-join the bank as a branch manager, the position he most enjoyed during his move up the ladder. He was welcomed back. Sheila retired three years later and received a generous pension. (She never heard from or about Jim Hardesty again.)

Winifred took over the position vacated by Sheila. She also founded and led a Family Recreation Club, which offered single parents and their children opportunities to go off for weekends and short trips together. Her Becka found Mr. Right, married him, and turned Winifred into a grandmother.

Judy left the company a few months after the takeover, to return to law school and follow her dream. She had acquired and sold her house after Hank took off to join some buddies in a cross-country trucking business. Her current position is as a valuable member of the State Supreme Court, specializing in financial matters.

Terri went back to school part-time to work toward a bona fide MBA that would lead her on a clearer career path to team management. She graduated two springs after the Alices' coup and returned to the management staff at Stateside Savings.

Ann was chosen to head the new Human Resources Department, where she used her people skills to hire the best people and, therefore, seldom had to fire anyone. Her newly implemented Employees Manual refused to use the word "don't" and offered *guidelines* in place of *rules*. She also insisted that a coffee machine be available at all times for both staff and customers alike in all twenty-nine branches.

In the end, at least by the end of the first year, Stateside Savings Bank became the chief beneficiary. Stateside's business zoomed; profits went up; new business was attracted to the bank (happy tellers brought in more happy customers). The following Annual Meeting was attended by so many shareholders, they had to move it to the city's new convention hall!

Mr. Talcott held out until that meeting, then grandly announced his retirement to the television cameras.

Only one customer complaint has been registered at Stateside Savings Bank in the more than twenty years since the Alices Rebellion. (That complaint resulted from a misunderstanding of the way interest was figured on savings accounts. The complainant smiled all the way home.)

The perfect curtain closer would be "…and they lived happily ever after!" But we all know that this is a story about society, economics, and politics, and the world as it is today. There will always be performers and there will always be audiences.

Have you noticed that more and more audiences are becoming part of the performances?

(CURTAIN)

ABOUT THE AUTHOR

Val Dumond loves to write stories devoid of blood and guts, although the atmosphere at "Stateside Savings Bank" often felt as if plenty of tears replaced the gore. Oh yes, the author worked in a financial organization similar to Stateside in those years when women were butting their heads against the glass ceiling.

After being riffed during an economic turndown, Val chose to set up her own business, never to work for a "boss" again. She did just that, and now writes, edits, and works with writers to publish their books.

This rebellious what-if book asks the question, "What if a group of women worked under the very nose of a tyrant to upset his reign?" Here you read a daydream that has been repeated in one form or another in the United States since the Yanks rebelled against the Brits all those many years ago.

This author has one more dream: What if women in the U.S. were represented in the nation's Constitution, obtaining legal acknowledgment of their existence and contributions? Or have you heard about the Equal Rights Amendment?

Other Books by Val Dumond

NONFICTION
Are You Singing Your Song?
The Anarchist's Guide to Grammar
Grammar For Grownups
Elements of Nonsexist Usage
Just Words — The Us and Them Thing
SHEIT — A No-nonsense Guidebook
to Writing and Using Nonsexist Language
Doin' the Puyallup
Steilacoom's Church
Olympia Coloring Book

FICTION
Cloudbursts (Short Stories & Plays)
When Roosters Fly
Sugar, Spice, and Stone
Ahlam's Stories
How We Fought World War II
at William T. Sherman Elementary School
Mush On and Smile (a novel)

ANTHOLOGY
The Sun Never Rises
Dream Makers